*Book One of The Taravale Series*

# EMILY FRASER

# WHAT THE
# LAND KEEPS

What the Land Keeps

Book One of The Taravale Series

Copyright © 2026 Emily Fraser





This is a work of fiction. Names, characters, places, and incidents are the product of the author's imagination or are used fictitiously. Any resemblance to actual persons, living or dead, or real events is coincidental.


First edition 2026


Published by Southern Ground Press, Australia


ISBN (paperback): 978-0-6455623-7-8

ISBN (ebook): 978-0-6455623-8-5

Printed in Australia

*For everyone who understands
what it means to come home.*

# CHAPTER ONE

The ute crested the last rise and the valley opened like a held breath.

Alice slowed without meaning to. The road here had always done that to her - demanded attention in a way the highways never had. A ribbon of bitumen turned to gravel, gravel to ruts, and then the old track that locals called a road only out of kindness. The tyres whispered over stones. Dust lifted behind her in a slow, patient plume.

Taravale sat somewhere behind her now, tucked into its dip of land with its pub, its single street and its habit of watching. She hadn't driven through the middle. She'd taken the back way in, as if that changed anything. As if the town didn't already know.

The gums thickened as the track dipped. Grey-green canopies knitted together overhead, and the light began to strobe through leaves - bright, dim, bright - until her eyes ached with remembering.

The creek line ran parallel to the road for a stretch, hidden but audible, a thin ribbon of water talking to itself. It had always sounded like this. Like it knew something.

She rolled the window down a fraction, just enough to let the smell in.

Eucalypt. Damp earth. Old timber warming in late-summer sun. And underneath it all, a faint mineral coldness that didn't belong to the day.

Stone.

Her fingers tightened on the steering wheel.

The farmhouse came into view through the trees - not as a reveal, but as an inevitability. One moment there was bush, scrub, fence posts. The next, the dark shape of the house was there, lodged between gum trunks as if it had been built by accident.

It looked smaller than it did in her memory, and older in a way that didn't match the years. The stone walls were darker than she remembered, mottled with shadow and lichen. The verandah wrapped around the front, its posts leaning ever so slightly, as if even the timber was tired. One corner caught full sun, bright and honeyed. The rest sat in shade, cool and unreadable.

A contradiction.

Alice killed the engine at the gate and sat for a moment with her hands in her lap, listening to the sudden quiet.

No engine. No radio. No phone signal ping.

Just the creek. The leaves. The far-off call of a bird she couldn't name. The faint ticking of the ute cooling down, metal contracting.

Comfort, her body supplied, without asking her permission.

And then, almost on top of it: unease.

She reached for her phone out of habit. One bar. Then none. She let it drop back into the cup holder like it had betrayed her. Her keys felt heavy in her palm.

She forced herself out of the ute.

Heat struck her first, the kind that lived close to the ground and rose in waves off dry grass. She shut the door and stood with her boots on the gravel, looking at the gate.

It was open.

Not wide. Not inviting. Just... unlatched, sitting half a handspan away from where it should have been, the chain hanging loose.

Alice stared at it, waiting for logic to arrive.

Maybe the last person through didn't bother. Maybe the wind had worked it. Maybe she had forgotten- no. She hadn't been here in twelve years. There was no "forgotten."

She walked to it slowly. The post was rough beneath her hand, worn smooth in places by decades of palms. The latch should have been down. It wasn't. The chain was looped, but not hooked.

She could see the tyre marks in the dust. One set, narrow. Hers.

No fresh tracks through the grass beyond.

"Don't," she muttered, because her brain had already begun to pull patterns out of nothing. A gate unlatched. A house in shade. The human need to make meaning.

She latched it anyway. The metal clicked with a sound that was far too final in the quiet. The chain clinked as she hooked it.

A small act. Something to do with her hands.

The gravel drive curved up toward the house. The yard, once a patchwork of fenced spaces and neat lines, had softened at the edges. Scrubby grass grew between stones. A few thistles had claimed a corner near the tank stand. The gumtrees were bigger than she remembered - or perhaps she was simply smaller in the ways that mattered now.

There were no animals in the front paddock. No movement except a pair of galahs lifting from the ground in a pink- grey burst as she crossed the yard. The sound of their wings was loud, then gone.

The front steps were uneven. Alice took them carefully, one hand on the verandah post. The timber creaked under her weight as if it resented being reminded it still had work to do.

The front door stood in shadow.

She remembered it as bright. Honey- coloured. A door you could see from the yard like a promise.

Now it was dark, the wood deepened with age, the iron handle dull. The old key sat in her pocket like a stone of its own. She pulled it out, held it for a second, then slid it into the lock.

It turned with reluctance. A dry scrape. The kind of sound you feel in your teeth.

The door swung inward, and the house breathed out something cold.

Not supernatural. Not dramatic. Just the natural cool of thick stone and rooms that didn't see enough sun - and the smell of it.

Damp. Dust. Faint mould. Old smoke trapped in walls. And- because of course - lavender, barely there, a ghost of something her mother used to hang in bunches from the rafters.

Alice stepped inside and shut the door behind her.

The sitting room was exactly as she remembered. The same heavy stone fireplace. The same small window that let in a shaft of light angled and thin. The same rug - not the same rug, but the memory of it in the pattern of dust on the floorboards.

Her eyes adjusted slowly.

There was furniture, covered in sheets. Ghost shapes. A table. A couch. A chair that could have been the one her father sat in to remove splinters from her knees with patient fingers.

She stood in the doorway until her heartbeat stopped trying to climb out of her throat.

"Just... look," she told herself. "Inventory. Practical. You're here to settle an estate. That's it."

She crossed the room. Her footsteps were quiet, swallowed by old timber.

A small draft moved through the room, lifting the edge of a sheet. She caught it automatically, pressed it back down, and her fingers brushed something underneath - wood, cool and smooth, with the shape of an armrest.

The house was alive with details like that. The kind of place that required your hands as much as your eyes.

She made her way down the hallway. It was darker here. The stone walls drew light into themselves. The air changed - cooler, damper. The corridor seemed longer than it should have been, as if the house expanded when you weren't looking.

The first door on the left was closed.

That hadn't been right. In her memory, that door was always open. That room always watched the hallway like an unblinking eye.

She stopped in front of it, listening.

Nothing.

No movement. No rustle. No mouse in the walls. Just the creek outside, faint through stone.

Her hand hovered over the handle.

She didn't open it.

Not yet.

A sensible part of her brain tried to catalogue. The door was closed because someone closed it. Estates get shut up. People cover furniture. People... make things neat when grief is too big for anything else.

Still.

She moved on, toward the kitchen, following the faintest hint of light.

And there it was - the contradiction. The shift. The place where the house stopped feeling like a memory trap and started feeling like a home.

The kitchen was bright.

A big window over the sink looked out onto the back paddock and the line of gums beyond. Sun poured in, turning dust motes into something almost pretty. The old wooden table sat in the centre, scarred with knife marks and stained rings and a thousand mornings. A bowl rested on the bench, empty. A tea towel hung from a hook, stiff and faded.

It shouldn't have looked so... lived in.

Alice set her bag down on the table, unzipped it, pulled out a bottle of water. The cap snapped in the quiet. She drank, and the water tasted faintly of plastic and relief.

She reached for her phone again without thinking and watched the screen search for service like it could conjure it out of stubbornness. Nothing.

She exhaled slowly and tried to ignore the pulse of anxiety in her throat.

She wasn't a child anymore. She was not trapped here. She had a car. She had money. She had a life built out of distance and coping and being sensible.

She could leave any time she wanted.

That thought should have steadied her.

Instead it made something twist.

There was a sound outside - metal against metal.

Alice froze mid-breath.

Not loud. Not dramatic. A small clink, like a chain settling.

Her eyes lifted to the kitchen window.

The back yard was empty. Sunlit. Still.

Then she saw it.

The back gate - the one that led to the creek track - was moving, just slightly, as if someone had pushed it and let it swing.

Alice set the water down carefully, as though any sudden movement might make a mistake real.

Her heartbeat started again, quick and shallow.

The gate swung once more and bumped gently against the post.

Clink.

No wind. The leaves on the gums were barely stirring.

She moved to the window.

Her reflection stared back at her over the glass - pale, tense, older than the last time she'd seen herself in this place. Behind it, the yard lay bright and ordinary. Nothing moved. No figure. No shadow between the trees.

She listened harder.

The creek.

The soft hush of leaves.

And then, faintly, from somewhere closer than it should have been —

Footsteps on verandah boards.

Slow. Unhurried. Familiar.

Alice's throat went dry.

She didn't turn right away. She stared at the yard, at the gate that had stopped moving, at the sunlight that made everything look like it couldn't possibly hold danger.

The footsteps paused.

A knock sounded on the back door.

Not aggressive.

Not polite.

Just... there.

Three taps, measured, as if whoever stood outside already knew she was in the kitchen.

Alice swallowed once, then put her hand on the edge of the sink and forced herself to speak.

"Who is it?"

For a beat, there was only the sound of the house holding its breath with her.

Then a man's voice, low and steady, came through the timber.

"Alice."

Her name hit her like a hand to the chest.

She closed her eyes, just for a second, and let the inevitable settle into place.

Because of course the town already knew.

And of course he did too.

She opened her eyes and stared at the back door, at the old brass handle, at the thin line of shadow underneath it.

"Tom," she said, and the fact that her voice didn't shake felt like a lie.

On the other side, he exhaled - she could hear it, like he was closer than the door suggested. Like the house carried sound differently on purpose.

"I saw dust on the road," he said. "Thought I'd better check the place was... right."

Alice's gaze flicked to the back gate in the yard.

Right.

Her fingers tightened on the sink edge.

She didn't answer immediately.

Because she didn't know what "right" meant here anymore.

And because the house, cool and quiet behind her, felt like it was listening too.

"Just a minute," she said finally.

She moved to the door and put her hand on the handle.

Cold metal. Familiar weight.

A comfort.

A warning.

She hesitated - just long enough to feel the shape of the story settling around her shoulders - and then she opened it.

# CHAPTER TWO

Tom stood on the verandah like he belonged to it.

Not leaning. Not looming. Just there - boots planted, shoulders easy, hands loose at his sides. The late- afternoon light caught in his hair and turned the dust on his shirt almost gold. He looked exactly as Alice remembered and nothing like the man she'd spent twelve years not thinking about.

"Hi," he said, as if they'd passed each other only yesterday.

She kept her hand on the door, half a barrier, half a brace. "You don't knock much anymore?"

His mouth twitched. "I knocked."

"You announced yourself."

"Didn't want to scare you."

Something sharp slid through her chest. She stepped back, letting the door swing wider. "Too late."

Tom's gaze flicked past her into the kitchen. He nodded once, satisfied, then looked back at her.

"You on your own?" he asked.

"Yes." She hated how defensive it sounded.

He seemed to hear it anyway. "Didn't say you weren't allowed to be."

She stepped aside. "You may as well come in. You're already halfway."

The verandah boards creaked as he crossed the threshold. The house seemed to register him - a shift in air, a change in pressure - like it recognised his weight. Alice felt it too, an old awareness settling under her skin.

Tom paused just inside, eyes adjusting. "Smells the same."

"Lavender and damp regret?" she offered.

"Stone," he said. "Old smoke. Water in the walls."

Of course he'd say that. He always named things the way they actually were.

She shut the door behind him, the sound too loud in the kitchen's quiet. "I only just got here."

"I know." He glanced at the table. Her bag. The open water bottle. "Didn't want to leave you long if something was... off."

Her pulse picked up. "Off how?"

He didn't answer straight away. Instead, he moved to the window and looked out at the yard, one hand braced lightly on the sill. Not casual. Not tense. Alert.

"Back gate," he said finally. "Was swinging."

Alice folded her arms. "I saw it."

"Wind's wrong for that."

"There was no wind."

He nodded, as if she'd passed a test. "That's what I thought."

She felt suddenly foolish for how much relief that brought. "The front gate was open too."

His head came around sharply. "Open- open, or just not latched?"

"Not latched."

His jaw set. "That gate doesn't do that."

She studied him, the familiar set of his shoulders when something didn't sit right. "So it's not just the house playing tricks."

"No." He turned fully toward her now. "It's not."

The kitchen seemed smaller with him in it. Warmer too, though that might have been her imagination. Or the way his presence grounded the space, the way it always had.

"Estate agent didn't mention anything unusual," she said.

"They wouldn't," Tom replied. "Not unless it affected the price."

She huffed a quiet laugh. "Some things never change."

"Some do." His eyes held hers for a beat longer than necessary.

She looked away first.

"Have you checked inside?" he asked.

"A little."

"And?"

"And I found the kitchen where it always was, and a hallway that feels longer than it should, and a door that's closed when it shouldn't be."

His expression shifted. "Which door?"

She hesitated. "The old bedroom."

He didn't pretend not to know which one she meant.

"That room's been shut for years," he said carefully.

"Not when I was a kid."

"No," he agreed. "Not then."

The silence stretched, thick with things neither of them wanted to be the first to touch.

Tom cleared his throat. "You eating tonight?"

She blinked. "What?"

"You look like you drove straight through." His gaze dropped briefly to her hands, to the faint tremor she hadn't noticed until he did. "There's food at the pub. Or Mara's van is still parked near the hall if you want something easier."

"Mara?" The name tugged at something half-remembered.

"Bell," he said. "Single mum. Coffee van. Parks wherever people need caffeine or an excuse to talk."

Alice smiled despite the tension. "Sounds about right."

"She keeps an eye on things," Tom added. "Sees patterns."

Her stomach tightened. "You all do that here, don't you?"

He met her look steadily. "You don't survive out here if you don't."

She sighed and leaned back against the bench. "I didn't come back to stir anything up."

"I know."

"I'm just here to sort the place. Sign papers. Decide what to do with it."

He nodded again, slow. "And then?"

"And then I leave."

The words landed harder than she expected. Tom's face didn't change, but something behind his eyes did - a closing, a settling.

"Right," he said. "Well. Until then."

"Until then," she echoed.

Another quiet stretch. The house hummed softly around them - the faint tick of cooling stone, the distant rush of the creek. Alice realised she was holding her breath again.

Tom straightened. "I'll walk the perimeter before I go. Check fences, gates. Make sure nothing's been interfered with."

"You don't have to—"

"I know," he interrupted gently. "But I will."

She swallowed her pride along with the knot in her throat. "Thank you."

He gave her a half- smile. "You always did hate needing help."

"And you always offered it anyway."

"Someone had to."

They shared a look - not romantic, not safe, but threaded with something old and unresolved.

Tom moved toward the back door, then paused. "If anything feels wrong tonight," he said, without turning around, "you call me. Day or night."

"I might not have reception."

He nodded. "Then you use the landline."

She frowned. "The landline?"

His smile this time was faint and knowing. "Old houses keep their secrets, Alice. But they also keep their connections."

He opened the door and stepped out onto the verandah. The boards creaked under his boots as he moved away, footsteps steady and unhurried.

Alice stood in the kitchen long after the sound faded, listening to the house settle again.

Outside, somewhere near the creek, a gate clinked softly.

She didn't go to look.

Not yet.

# CHAPTER THREE

Tom took the long way around the house.

Not because he enjoyed it - though there was comfort in the familiar rhythm of boots on dirt - but because you learned more that way. Straight lines missed things. The land didn't.

The side paddock gate was latched properly. Chain hooked. Rust where it always was. He crouched, fingers brushing the ground beneath it. Dust disturbed, but not fresh. Older. Days, maybe. Not today.

He stood slowly, eyes lifting to the tree line.

The gums closest to the house were ancient, their trunks pale and scarred, limbs stretching wide like they'd claimed the place before anyone bothered to build on it. One of them had dropped a branch recently -  a decent- sized limb, splintered where it had hit the ground. Tom frowned.

That hadn't been there yesterday.

He crossed to it and crouched again, studying the break. Clean enough to be recent. The ground beneath was scuffed, bark fragments scattered in a way that suggested it hadn't fallen straight down.

He straightened and followed the line of damage back up the trunk.

Someone had climbed it.

Not recently - the marks weren't fresh - but not years ago either. The bark was disturbed where boots or hands had scraped, just enough to tell a story if you knew how to look.

Tom swore under his breath.

He moved on, circling toward the back paddock and the creek track. The grass here was longer, uncut. Alice's family had always let it grow this time of year, said it kept the ground cooler. The fence ran crooked along the boundary, posts leaning at angles that would have bothered anyone new to the place.

Tom knew which ones to worry about.

He stopped near the back gate.

It was latched now. Chain secured. No movement.

He crouched, fingers brushing the post, the latch, the ground beneath. The soil was darker here, still holding a little moisture from the creek. Footprints would be obvious.

There were two sets.

One was Alice's - lighter, the pattern of her boots familiar even after all this time. The other was heavier. Longer stride. Someone who knew the gate well enough not to rush.

Tom's jaw tightened.

He stood and followed the tracks a short way before they disappeared into scrub and leaf litter. Whoever it was hadn't come from the creek itself. They'd approached from the east, keeping to the trees, staying out of sight of the house.

Someone who didn't want to be seen arriving.

Tom straightened and scanned the bush. Nothing moved. No birds startled. No cattle restless. The land was calm in a way that meant something had already happened, not that nothing was wrong.

He turned back toward the house.

From this angle, he could see Alice through the kitchen window. She stood at the sink, arms folded, staring out into the yard as if willing it to explain itself. The light caught her hair, showed the silver she'd earned. She looked smaller than she used to. Or maybe the house just did that to people - stripped them back.

Tom exhaled slowly.

Twelve years. And the land still put them in the same places.

He checked the old dairy ruins next - stone walls collapsed inward, roof long gone. A good place to watch without being seen. Nothing obvious there, but the grass was pressed down near one wall, flattened just enough to suggest someone had stood there recently.

Watching the house.

Tom moved on, faster now. The shearing shed was next - doors hanging crooked, one hinge rusted through. He pushed it open and stepped inside, the smell of old lanolin and dust hitting him immediately. Light slanted through broken boards. Nothing disturbed. No fresh tracks.

Still, he stood there longer than necessary, listening.

The land didn't lie, but it didn't shout either.

By the time he made it back to the verandah, his shoulders were tight with the weight of what he hadn't told her. He paused at the bottom step, eyes lifting to the house.

Alice stood just inside the doorway now, arms crossed, watching him. Not anxious exactly - alert. The way she'd always been when she sensed trouble but refused to let it own her.

He climbed the steps and stopped a pace away from her.

"Everything okay?" she asked.

"Mostly."

She lifted an eyebrow. "That's not comforting."

He considered his words. "Front gate didn't open itself."

Her lips pressed together. "I thought so."

"Someone's been around," he continued. "Not today, necessarily. But recently."

A flicker crossed her face - fear, anger, something harder to name. "Around the house?"

"Yes."

She inhaled sharply, then steadied. "Why?"

Tom didn't answer straight away. He glanced past her, down the dark hallway, toward the closed door they'd both avoided naming.

"Because people don't forget this place," he said finally. "And some of them don't forgive it either."

Her gaze followed his. "You're not going to tell me to leave, are you?"

"No," he said. "I'm going to tell you to be careful."

She let out a breath that sounded almost like a laugh. "That's new."

"Is it?" His mouth twitched. "You were always careful. You just didn't call it that."

They stood there, the house humming softly around them.

"Stay tonight," he said suddenly.

Her head snapped up. "What?"

"Not here," he clarified quickly. "At my place. Just until we work out what's going on."

She shook her head. "No. I won't do that."

"I figured," he said. "But I had to ask."

She hesitated. "You'll check in tomorrow?"

"I will." He met her eyes. "And tonight, you lock every door. Front and back. Use the bolt on the hallway door if you need to."

"The hallway door?"

"The one that sticks," he said. "Still does."

She swallowed. "You remember that."

"I remember most things that matter."

Silence settled between them, weighted but not heavy.

Tom stepped back, giving her space. "I'll leave the ute near the track tonight," he said. "If anything happens, you won't be alone."

She studied him for a long moment, then nodded once. "Thank you."

He tipped his head in acknowledgement and turned away.

As he stepped off the verandah, Alice called after him.

"Tom?"

He turned.

"If you find out who's been here..." Her voice wavered, then steadied. "You'll tell me?"

He held her gaze. "I won't lie to you."

It wasn't a promise of safety. But it was the truth.

He walked away, boots steady on gravel, already listening to the land as if it might answer him now.

Behind him, Alice closed the door.

The latch slid into place.

Inside, the house settled around her - cool stone, dark corners, light- filled rooms - holding its contradictions close.

And somewhere beyond the trees, unseen, someone else was listening too.

# CHAPTER FOUR

Alice locked the door twice.

Not because she forgot she'd already done it - she was annoyingly sure of that - but because the sound of the bolt sliding home felt like something she could anchor herself to. Metal into metal. A decision made.

She moved through the house methodically, switching on lamps rather than overhead lights, letting pools of warmth settle where they would. The sitting room stayed dim no matter what she did. The stone drank light like it was thirsty for it.

She left that room alone.

In the hallway, she hesitated at the narrow door halfway down. The one Tom had mentioned. The one that stuck.

She hadn't meant to go there yet. Had told herself she'd wait until morning, until daylight stripped the place of its shadows and made courage easier to pretend. But now the thought of leaving it untouched felt worse than opening it.

She pressed her palm flat against the timber.

Cold.

The handle resisted when she turned it, just as Tom had said it would. She leaned her weight into it and felt it give with a reluctant groan, the hinges complaining like they were offended by the interruption.

The room beyond was smaller than she remembered.

Or maybe she'd grown.

The air was different here - heavier, damp enough that it sat on her skin. The curtains were drawn, the fabric thick and faded. A single narrow bed hugged the far wall, its frame iron and rusted at the joints. No sheets. Just a bare mattress, mottled with age.

This had been her grandmother's room, once. Later, it had been no one's. The place where furniture went to be forgotten. The room everyone pretended didn't exist.

Alice stood in the doorway and waited for the rush of memory.

It didn't come.

Instead, there was a strange, hollow calm. Like whatever this room had held had already been spent.

She stepped inside.

The floorboards creaked softly under her weight. She crossed to the window and pulled the curtain back an inch, just enough to let in a stripe of fading daylight. Outside, the gums cast long shadows across the ground, the creek line hidden but audible.

She turned slowly, taking the room in with adult eyes.

There was a wardrobe against one wall, its door slightly ajar. A chest at the foot of the bed. Dust everywhere, thick enough to write your name in if you were inclined toward sentimentality.

She wasn't.

Alice opened the wardrobe.

It was empty except for a single hook screwed into the timber - the kind used to hang coats or hats. Or heavier things, once.

She closed it again.

The chest creaked when she lifted the lid. Inside were papers - yellowed, curled at the edges, tied together with twine that had once been white. Letters. Receipts. A folded map with creases worn into it by repetition.

She didn't touch them.

Not yet.

This wasn't the night for that kind of truth.

She closed the lid carefully and stepped back into the hallway, pulling the door shut behind her. This time, she slid the bolt across without hesitation.

The click echoed more loudly than it should have.

She moved faster after that, checking the remaining doors, securing windows, grounding herself in small, practical acts. When she reached the kitchen again, the light outside had shifted to that soft, uncertain hour where day gives up without fully surrendering.

She heated soup from a can and ate standing at the bench, spoon clinking quietly against ceramic. The normality of it felt almost obscene in the middle of everything else.

After, she washed the bowl, dried it, and set it upside down on the rack.

She wasn't tired, exactly. But her body felt heavy, like it was bracing for something it didn't have a name for.

Alice carried her bag into the back living room and settled on the couch with a throw pulled around her shoulders. The firebox sat cold and unused. She didn't light it. Fire demanded attention. Tonight, she wanted stillness.

Outside, night gathered slowly.

The bush changed its voice after dark. Day birds fell quiet. Something else took over - insects, distant movement, the low rustle of leaves that made every sound feel closer than it was.

She checked her phone again. No service. She set it face down on the table and tried not to think about how easily the world could narrow to the reach of her own arms out here.

A sound carried through the house.

Not loud. Not sudden.

A door, somewhere deeper in the structure, shifting on its hinges.

Alice's breath caught.

She sat very still, listening.

The sound came again - a soft scrape, followed by the unmistakable thump of wood settling back into place.

Her gaze flicked toward the hallway.

The bolt on the old bedroom door was still across. She could see the shadow of it from where she sat.

This wasn't that.

The sound came once more, closer this time. From the sitting room.

Her pulse hammered in her ears. She rose slowly, every nerve alight, and moved toward the doorway of the back living room. The house felt larger at night, its spaces stretching and contracting in ways that made distance unreliable.

She reached the edge of the room and peered down the hallway.

The sitting room door was open.

She was certain she'd left it closed.

The lamp inside cast a low, amber glow across the threshold, light spilling into the hallway like something that had escaped.

Alice stood frozen, every instinct screaming at once.

Then she saw it.

The sheet that covered the armchair - the one she'd pressed down earlier - had been pulled back.

Not much. Just enough to expose the curve of the wooden arm beneath.

Her mind raced through explanations. Draft. Settling. The house breathing.

But the air was still.

She took one step forward.

The floorboard creaked.

The light in the sitting room flickered.

And then, very softly, from somewhere just beyond the doorway, she heard it.

A breath.

Not hers.

Not the house's.

Human.

Alice didn't shout.

Didn't run.

She did the one thing that felt instinctively right.

She backed away, slow and silent, until her fingers brushed the edge of the kitchen bench. Her hand slid along it until it found the drawer where the old torch lived. She eased it open and wrapped her fingers around the cool metal.

The breath sounded again.

Closer now.

Alice flicked the torch on and aimed it straight down the hallway.

The beam cut through the dimness, harsh and white, lighting stone walls and doorframes and -

Nothing.

The sitting room was empty.

The chair sat where it always had. The sheet hung loose over its back, disturbed but not displaced.

The breath was gone.

Her heart slammed against her ribs.

She stood there for a long moment, torch trembling in her hand, waiting for something else to move.

Nothing did.

Finally, she lowered the torch and exhaled shakily.

"You're imagining things," she whispered. "Old houses make noise."

But even as she said it, she knew.

This hadn't been the house.

Alice locked herself into the back living room that night.

She dragged the couch across the doorway just far enough to make noise if it moved. She kept the torch beside her, her phone within reach, the windows shut tight despite the heat.

Sleep came in short, fractured pieces.

Each time she drifted, the same thought surfaced, unbidden and insistent:

Someone had been inside the house with her.

And they'd left without taking anything at all.

# CHAPTER FIVE

Alice woke before dawn with her heart already racing.

For a few seconds, she didn't know why - only that her body was braced, muscles tight, breath shallow. The back living room lay in that grey hour where shapes existed but refused clarity. The couch pressed against the doorway exactly as she'd left it. The torch sat on the floor beside her hand.

Nothing had moved.

Nothing had happened.

She lay there anyway, listening.

The house was quieter at this hour than it had been all night. No insects. No wind. Even the creek seemed to have lowered its voice, as if it too were waiting.

Alice pushed herself upright slowly, joints stiff from sleeping half- curled, and checked the doorway. The couch hadn't shifted. No scrape marks on the floor. No sign of interference.

Her pulse eased, reluctantly.

You didn't imagine breath, she told herself. But you also didn't see anything. Which meant -

She stopped that line of thinking before it could finish.

Daylight would fix this. Daylight always did.

She stood, stretched the ache from her shoulders, and moved the couch back into place. The floorboards complained softly, but nothing else answered. She cracked the door open and peered into the hallway.

Stillness.

The sitting room door stood exactly where it had been last night - open, the lamp still on. Its light had dulled to a faint amber glow in the growing morning.

Alice crossed the hallway carefully and shut it, turning the lamp off before she could talk herself out of it. The room felt different in daylight - smaller, less watchful - but she didn't linger.

In the kitchen, the sky beyond the window was just beginning to pale. She filled the kettle from the tap, listening to the rush of water like it was proof of something normal still existing. When it clicked on, the sound felt indecently loud.

She made tea this time. Strong. Familiar.

Steam curled upward, fogging the window slightly, and she wiped it away with the back of her hand. Outside, the yard looked untouched. Dew clung to grass. The gumtrees stood motionless, their pale trunks glowing faintly.

The back gate was shut.

Latched.

Alice stared at it for a long moment.

She was certain - absolutely certain - that she hadn't checked it after Tom left. Hadn't gone anywhere near it after dark. Hadn't stepped outside at all.

Someone had.

Her phone buzzed on the table, sudden and sharp.

She flinched, tea sloshing dangerously close to the rim of the mug, then grabbed the phone.

One bar of reception flickered into existence.

A message came through.

**Tom:** You awake?

Relief hit her so hard she had to sit down.

She typed back quickly, thumbs clumsy.

**Alice:** Yes. Did you come back here last night?

The reply took longer than she liked.

She stared at the back gate through the window while she waited, every sense stretched thin.

The phone buzzed again.

**Tom:** No. Why?

Her chest tightened.

**Alice:** The gate's latched.

Three dots appeared. Disappeared. Appeared again.

**Tom:** It was latched when I left.

She swallowed.

**Alice:** It wasn't when I went to bed.

The dots paused for a long time this time.

**Tom:** I'm on my way.

Alice exhaled, the tension draining just enough to leave her shaky.

She moved through the house again, checking rooms with daylight on her side. Nothing was missing. Nothing was broken. But the sitting room chair now sat closer to the fireplace than she remembered.

She didn't trust her memory enough to say that aloud.

By the time she heard Tom's ute on the track, the sun had lifted fully above the trees. The sound grounded her - familiar engine note, steady approach. She stepped onto the verandah as he pulled up near the gate.

He climbed out, eyes already scanning, posture alert without being frantic.

"Morning," he said.

"Someone was here," she replied.

He didn't argue.

They walked the perimeter together this time. Tom crouched, studied the ground, the gate, the latch. His silence stretched, heavy with concentration.

Finally, he straightened. "They came in from the creek side again. Same approach. Careful."

Alice folded her arms against the morning chill. "Why not take something? If they wanted to scare me, last night was enough."

"They didn't want you gone," Tom said quietly.

She looked at him. "How do you know that?"

"Because if they wanted you gone, they'd make it obvious. Break a window. Kill power. Leave a message you couldn't ignore." He met her eyes. "This is watching. Measuring."

Her skin prickled.

"Someone wants you to stay," he continued. "Or at least wants to see what you do next."

Alice thought of the closed bedroom. The chest. The papers she hadn't opened.

The land didn't keep secrets on its own.

People put them there.

She looked back at the house - the stone walls, the light- filled kitchen, the dark rooms that waited.

"I think," she said slowly, "they're afraid of what I might find."

Tom's jaw tightened. "Then we're asking the right questions."

Alice nodded, a quiet resolve settling into place.

She hadn't come back to Taravale to dig up the past.

But it seemed the past had already decided to meet her.

# CHAPTER SIX

Tom insisted on checking the house.

Not with the urgency of someone chasing a threat, but with the thoroughness of someone who knew how easily small things got missed. He moved room to room while Alice followed a step behind, watching him see what she hadn't known to look for.

He didn't touch much. Doors, mostly. Hinges. Latches. Window frames. He paused longer in places where the stone walls pressed close, where the air stayed cool even now that the day had warmed.

"This one," he said quietly, stopping at the sitting room door.

Alice's stomach tightened. "That's where - "

"I know," he said, not looking at her. He stepped inside and stood still, listening.

The room felt different in daylight, but not enough to make her forget the way it had felt last night. The chair sat angled toward the fireplace. The sheet lay folded over its back, not draped.

Tom crouched beside it.

"Someone sat here," he said.

Alice blinked. "How can you tell?"

He tapped the edge of the rug with two fingers. "Indentation. It's faint, but it's there. Weight pressed down, then lifted." He glanced up at her. "Not long. They didn't stay."

Her throat went dry. "They were... comfortable enough to sit?"

"Comfortable enough to wait."

He stood and crossed to the fireplace, running his hand along the stone mantle. His fingers paused at a point where the dust had been disturbed.

"Here too," he murmured.

"For what?"

He straightened slowly. "Someone leaned here. Watched the hallway."

Alice's gaze slid involuntarily to the corridor beyond the door - long, dim, leading straight to the kitchen. To her.

She wrapped her arms around herself. "So they weren't just wandering."

"No," Tom said. "They were deliberate."

They moved on.

In the kitchen, he checked the back door, the latch, the frame. "This was opened quietly," he said. "No force. They've done it before."

Alice swallowed. "When?"

He hesitated. "Hard to say."

She read what he wasn't saying anyway. Before she came back. Before anyone thought to worry.

They reached the hallway and stopped at the closed door.

Tom didn't touch it. He just stood there, studying the bolt.

"You went in," he said.

"Yes."

"You didn't open the chest."

Her head snapped up. "How do you know that?"

"Because if you had, you'd be asking different questions."

A chill ran through her. "What's in there?"

"Paper," he said. "History. And probably the reason someone doesn't want you settling this place too quickly."

Alice stared at the door, at the timber worn smooth by generations of hands. "You've known about it all along."

"I knew there were things," he said carefully. "I didn't know how much."

"Did anyone else?"

"Some," he admitted. "Not everyone. And not all the same things."

She exhaled slowly. "Taravale's favourite trick."

"Keeping truth in pieces," Tom said. "So no one feels responsible for the whole."

They went upstairs next. The staircase complained loudly, but Tom didn't slow. He checked the bedrooms, the storage room, the trunks pushed against the wall. He lifted lids, shifted boxes, examined the dust like it might speak.

When he finally stepped back into the hallway, his expression had changed.

"They didn't come up here," he said.

"Why not?"

"Because there's nothing here they care about." He met her gaze. "Whatever they want is downstairs."

They returned to the kitchen, the light now bright enough to feel almost intrusive. Alice poured fresh water into the kettle without asking if he wanted tea. He didn't object.

They stood at the bench while it boiled.

"Tom," she said finally. "Why me?"

He didn't answer straight away. When he did, his voice was low. "Because you can sell this place."

Her hand stilled on the mug. "Anyone could."

"Yes," he said. "But you won't - not without understanding what you're selling."

She looked at him. "You think they're afraid I'll keep it."

"I think they're afraid you'll look too closely."

The kettle clicked off. Steam rose between them.

Alice poured the water and watched the leaves bloom in the cup like something coming back to life.

"I'm not leaving," she said quietly.

Tom studied her face. "I didn't think you would."

"I need to know what's in that chest."

He nodded. "Then we don't do it alone."

She raised an eyebrow. "You volunteering?"

"I'm insisting."

She hesitated, then gave a small, wry smile. "You always did."

A sound drifted in through the open window - an engine, distant but approaching. Alice stiffened.

Tom moved instantly, gaze flicking toward the yard. "That'll be Mara."

"Coffee van Mara?"

"Mm." His mouth twitched. "She doesn't come up here unless she means to."

They stepped onto the verandah together. Down near the gate, the coffee van pulled to a stop, dust settling around it. Mara Bell climbed out, one hand shading her eyes as she looked toward the house.

She saw them and lifted a hand in greeting.

Tom's shoulders eased slightly. "Good. She'll have seen something."

Alice followed his gaze back to the house for just a moment - the stone walls, the open windows, the rooms that held their silence close.

Whatever was buried here had been patient.

It could wait a little longer.

But not much.

# CHAPTER SEVEN

Mara didn't waste time.

She crossed the yard with the purposeful stride of someone used to reading a room before she entered it, eyes flicking from the verandah to the trees to the back paddock as if the order mattered. The coffee van idled near the gate, a low, familiar hum that felt almost out of place against the house's older, quieter sounds.

"Morning," she said, stopping at the bottom step. Her smile was brief but genuine. "You look like someone who didn't sleep."

Alice let out a breath that might have been a laugh. "I slept. Technically."

Mara's gaze shifted to Tom. "She wasn't alone, was she."

Tom shook his head. "Not entirely."

Mara nodded once, as if that confirmed something she'd already suspected. She climbed the steps and leaned lightly against a verandah post, arms folded. "I saw the gate open last night," she said. "Late. Later than anyone should've been wandering."

Alice's stomach tightened. "You didn't stop?"

"I didn't see a person," Mara replied calmly. "Just the movement. Thought it was stock at first, but the timing was wrong." Her eyes met Alice's. "And then I saw your light come on."

Alice swallowed. "So someone was here."

"Yes." Mara's voice softened slightly. "And they knew you were."

Silence settled between them, thick with the weight of it.

Mara broke it first. "You planning on opening whatever it is you're pretending isn't in this house?"

Alice blinked. "How did you - "

"Because people don't watch empty places," Mara said. "They watch change."

Tom exhaled through his nose. "We were going to look. Together."

"Good," Mara said. "Because if you don't, someone else will."

Alice glanced between them. "You're both very calm about this."

Mara smiled faintly. "I run a coffee van in a town where everyone thinks they're invisible. You learn quickly what matters."

She pushed off the post. "I can give you an hour. I told Jo I was heading out this way. She'll expect me back." A pause. "If I'm not, she'll start asking questions."

Tom nodded. "That helps."

They moved back inside, the house responding to their presence like it always did - with a subtle shift in air, a deepening of quiet. Alice led them down the hallway, her footsteps slower now, more deliberate.

The closed door waited.

She reached for the bolt and hesitated.

Mara watched her closely. "You don't have to open it today."

"Yes, I do," Alice said. Her hand slid the bolt free. The sound echoed sharply.

The door opened with the same reluctant groan as before.

The room looked different in full daylight. Less ominous. More... honest. Dust motes drifted lazily in the stripe of sun cutting across the floor. The iron bedframe caught the light, rust flaring dull orange.

Alice crossed to the chest and knelt, fingers resting on the lid.

"Letters," she said quietly. "Receipts. A map."

Tom crouched beside her. "Land titles?"

"Possibly."

Mara stayed near the door, eyes on the hallway behind them rather than the room itself. "People get strange about paper," she said. "Ink lasts longer than memory."

Alice lifted the lid.

The papers inside were neatly stacked, tied with twine gone brittle with age. She untied it carefully, the fibres crumbling under her fingers, and lifted the top letter free.

The handwriting was tight, controlled. Familiar in a way that made her chest ache.

"This is my grandfather's," she said. "But... not like his letters. This is formal. Careful."

Tom leaned closer. "Read it."

Alice scanned the page, her brow furrowing. "It's about boundaries. About creek access. About land that was never officially transferred."

Mara's head snapped up. "Millson land?"

Alice nodded slowly. "Part of it."

The room seemed to draw in around them.

Tom's jaw tightened. "That would explain a lot."

Alice flipped to the map. Pencil lines crisscrossed the paper, marking tracks, water points, fence lines that didn't match the modern layout. One section near the creek was circled heavily, notes written in the margin.

"Someone changed the boundaries," she said. "Quietly. Decades ago."

"And your family knew," Tom added.

"Yes." Her voice wavered. "Or at least... he did."

Mara shifted her weight. "That kind of knowledge makes people nervous. Especially if they've built their lives on the other version."

Alice closed her eyes briefly. The house felt closer now, its walls pressing in as if listening.

"This isn't just about me," she said. "Or the house."

"No," Tom agreed. "It's about who owns what - and who gets to decide."

A sound carried faintly through the open window. Not a vehicle. Not the wind.

A footstep.

Mara's head turned sharply toward the hallway. "We're not alone."

Tom rose in one smooth motion, positioning himself between Alice and the door.

The footstep came again. Closer this time.

Then a voice - unfamiliar, male, carefully neutral.

"Thought I might find someone home."

Alice's blood ran cold.

She knew that voice.

It belonged to someone who had every reason
to be afraid of what lay open on the bed behind her.

# CHAPTER EIGHT

Tom didn't move.

Not toward the door. Not toward the sound. He simply shifted his weight - a subtle adjustment that put his body squarely between Alice and the hallway, his presence solid and unmistakable.

Mara stayed where she was, one hand braced against the doorframe, the other casually resting on her hip. Anyone who didn't know her would mistake it for ease. Alice knew better now.

The footsteps stopped just outside the doorway.

"Well," the voice said again, closer now. "This is awkward."

Alice recognised it fully this time. The cadence. The confidence softened by civility. The way it assumed it belonged wherever it turned up.

"Gavin Millson," she said, before Tom could. Her voice surprised her - steady, even.

There was a pause.

Then a chuckle. "I was hoping it was you."

Tom's jaw tightened. "You don't come up here without a reason."

Gavin stepped into the doorway.

He was dressed neatly - clean jeans, pressed shirt, boots that had seen paddocks but not lately. His hair was greying at the temples, his smile polite enough to pass for friendly if you didn't look too closely.

His eyes went straight to the bed.

To the open chest.

To the papers spread between Alice's hands.

The smile faltered - just a fraction - then returned, careful and practiced.

"I heard you were back," he said. "Thought I'd check the place was... secure."

Mara snorted softly. "Funny way of doing it. Creeping around after dark."

Gavin's gaze flicked to her. "Evening, Mara. Or morning. You're everywhere these days."

"Someone has to be," she replied. "Town's been quiet lately."

"Quiet's good," Gavin said. "Quiet keeps things settled."

Alice stood slowly, the papers clutched to her chest. "Is that why you were here last night?"

The air sharpened.

Gavin's eyes met hers. "I was driving past. Saw a light. Thought I'd make sure you weren't spooked by the house settling."

Tom let out a low, humourless laugh. "You climbed a tree to do that?"

The smile dropped completely this time.

"I don't know what you think you saw," Gavin said, voice cooling, "but you're mistaken."

Tom stepped forward, just enough to claim space. "I know what I saw."

Mara crossed her arms. "And I know what I didn't. Which was any reason for you to be on this property at midnight."

Gavin exhaled slowly, as if indulging children. "Look. This house has history. It unsettles people. Always has. Alice's family included."

"Leave my family out of it," Alice snapped.

His gaze returned to her, softer now - too soft. "You don't need to go digging through old junk. It won't do you any good."

Her grip tightened on the papers. "You're afraid of what they say."

"I'm concerned," he corrected. "About misunderstandings."

Tom's voice cut in, sharp. "Land boundaries aren't misunderstandings."

Gavin's eyes flashed. "Those maps are obsolete."

"They're evidence," Alice said quietly.

For a moment, something ugly flickered across Gavin's face - anger, fear, calculation - then it was gone.

"You should be careful," he said. "Taravale doesn't take kindly to people stirring old grievances."

Mara raised an eyebrow. "Funny. Seems like Taravale's already stirred."

Gavin straightened, his tone firm. "I'm asking you to leave this alone."

"No," Alice said.

The word landed cleanly between them.

Gavin studied her, really looked this time. "You always were stubborn."

"And you always assumed that meant I'd back down eventually."

Silence stretched.

Finally, he nodded once. "Think about it."

He turned and walked down the hallway, his footsteps measured, unhurried - the sound of a man used to leaving without being stopped.

The front door opened.

Closed.

The house exhaled.

Alice sagged slightly, the adrenaline leaving her limbs weak. Tom reached out, steadying her without comment.

Mara let out a breath. "Well. That didn't take long."

Tom's eyes stayed on the hallway. "He won't stop."

Alice looked down at the papers in her hands - at the lines drawn by someone who'd known this would matter one day.

"Neither will I," she said.

Outside, the creek kept running.

And somewhere in Taravale, a silence that had held for decades had finally cracked.

# CHAPTER NINE

They didn't speak for a while after Gavin left.

The house settled back into itself, as if embarrassed by the outburst, stone ticking faintly as it adjusted to the heat of the day. Alice sat on the edge of the bed in the closed room, the papers spread across her lap now, her hands still trembling despite her best efforts to stop them.

Mara broke the silence first. "He didn't expect you to be holding those already."

Tom nodded. "That look wasn't irritation. It was surprise."

Alice stared at the map. "My grandfather knew."

"Yes," Tom said gently. "And he was careful."

Mara shifted her weight. "Careful people don't hide things unless they're afraid of who might find them."

Alice traced one of the pencil lines with her finger. It followed the creek, not the fence. Natural boundaries instead of surveyed ones. The kind of truth land remembered even when paperwork didn't.

"So what now?" she asked.

Tom leaned against the wall, arms crossed, thinking. "Now we slow down."

Mara snorted. "He won't."

"No," Tom agreed. "Which means we don't give him a reason to escalate."

Alice looked up sharply. "He already climbed trees and sat in my house."

"And now he's been seen," Tom said. "By all of us. That matters."

Mara nodded. "He'll shift tactics. People like him always do once they realise the quiet way didn't work."

Alice closed her eyes briefly. Her pulse still hadn't quite found its rhythm again. "I don't want this to turn ugly."

"It already has," Mara said softly. "It just hasn't bled yet."

That landed heavily.

Alice folded the papers back together with care and retied them with a length of twine from the kitchen drawer. She placed them back in the chest, but this time she didn't close the lid.

"I'm not pretending it isn't here anymore," she said.

Tom met her gaze. "Good."

Mara glanced toward the hallway. "I should go. If Gavin decides to mention this visit, it'll be easier if I was never here."

Alice frowned. "You're just going to leave me?"

Mara smiled - small, reassuring. "I'm going to sit in my van where everyone can see me. That's protection too."

She paused at the doorway. "And Alice?"

"Yes?"

"You didn't imagine last night."

Alice swallowed. "You're sure?"

Mara nodded. "He wanted you unsettled. Watching yourself. Questioning your instincts."

Alice felt a cold thread run down her spine.

After Mara left, the house felt quieter again - but no longer empty.

Tom stayed.

He made tea again without asking, moving around the kitchen with the ease of someone who'd done it a hundred times before. Alice watched him from the table, the ordinary domesticity of it grounding in a way she hadn't expected.

"You don't have to stay," she said.

"I know."

"But you are."

"Yes."

She let that sit between them, unexamined for now.

Later, when the afternoon stretched long and the heat pressed in through the windows, Tom walked the boundary again while Alice photographed the papers, sending copies to an old contact in town who owed her grandfather more than one favour.

Each click of the camera felt like a small act of defiance.

When Tom came back, his expression was grim. "Gavin's ute passed the gate twice."

"Slow?"

"Very."

Alice exhaled. "He's testing."

"He's reminding," Tom corrected. "He wants you to feel watched."

She looked out toward the creek, sunlight flashing on the water through the trees. "I do."

"Good," he said quietly. "Because awareness is safer than denial."

She turned to him. "You've been living with this your whole life, haven't you."

Tom hesitated. "With versions of it."

"Why didn't you say anything?"

He met her eyes. "Because until you came back, it was just history. Now it's personal."

The weight of that pressed in on her chest.

As evening crept closer, shadows lengthening across the yard, Alice felt the shift again - the subtle sense of something tightening, like the land itself was drawing a line.

She locked the doors early that night.

And this time, when darkness fell, she didn't pretend she was alone.

Because someone out there already knew she wasn't backing down.

And Taravale didn't forgive that easily.

# CHAPTER TEN

The first thing Alice noticed as night fell was how deliberately the dark arrived.

It didn't rush in like a storm. It edged closer, minute by minute, softening the line between paddock and bush until the distance blurred. The creek's voice deepened, the steady rush becoming something more insistent, like it was reminding the land it still moved even when everything else stilled.

Tom lit the fire just after sunset.

He didn't ask. Just stacked the wood neatly, struck the match, and coaxed the flame into being with practiced patience. The room warmed slowly, the stone releasing cold in stages, like it needed time to decide whether to trust the heat.

Alice watched from the arm of the couch, her knees pulled up, hands wrapped around a mug she'd stopped drinking from. The firelight softened

Tom's features, threw shadows she remembered too well across his face.

"You always did that," she said quietly.

"Did what?"

"Make things feel manageable without pretending they weren't dangerous."

He glanced at her. "Someone had to."

The words sat between them - not accusatory, not tender. Just true.

They ate a simple dinner, barely tasting it. Outside, something moved through the scrub - a wallaby, maybe - but both of them went still at the sound before relaxing again.

Tom checked the locks once more.

"Windows?" Alice asked.

"Secured," he said. "Except the small one in the sitting room. Frame's swollen. I wedged it."

"Good."

Silence settled in after that. Not awkward. Watchful.

Alice rose and crossed to the hallway, stopping in front of the closed door again. The bolt glinted faintly in the firelight.

"You don't have to look tonight," Tom said from behind her.

"I know."

She rested her palm against the timber anyway, grounding herself in the solid reality of it. "I think he knows what's in there. Maybe always did."

Tom nodded. "But knowing something exists isn't the same as knowing it'll be used."

Her shoulders squared. "It will be."

A faint smile touched his mouth. "That's the Alice I remember."

She turned back to him. "You didn't like her much."

"I loved her," he said simply. "She scared me."

The honesty in it stole her breath.

Before she could respond, a sharp crack echoed from outside.

Not thunder.

Not an animal.

Tom moved instantly, reaching for the torch by the door. "Stay here."

She followed anyway, stopping just inside the doorway as he stepped onto the verandah. The night air was cooler now, heavy with the smell of damp leaves.

The sound came again - wood snapping.

Tom swept the torch beam across the yard.

The fallen branch beneath the gumtree had been dragged.

Not far. Just enough to block the narrow track that led toward the creek.

Alice felt a cold certainty settle into her bones.

"He wants you to see," Tom said quietly. "This isn't about hiding anymore."

As if in answer, something reflective caught the torchlight near the branch.

A small object lay in the dirt.

Tom approached cautiously and crouched, lifting it with two fingers.

It was an old fence marker - rusted, bent, unmistakably from this property.

Tied to it with twine was a folded scrap of paper.

Alice's pulse roared in her ears. "Don't."

Tom unfolded it anyway.

Only four words were written there, in block letters, careful and controlled.

**THIS WAS NEVER YOURS.**

The night pressed closer.

Alice stepped forward, her voice steady despite the fear threading through it. "He's wrong."

Tom looked at her, something fierce and protective in his eyes. "And now he knows you know it too."

Somewhere beyond the trees, a bird cried out sharply and fell silent.

Alice stared into the dark, the message burning itself into her memory.

This wasn't a warning anymore.

It was a challenge.

And Taravale had just chosen its side.

# CHAPTER ELEVEN

Alice didn't sleep at all that night.

She lay on the couch with the fire burned down to embers, the message replaying itself over and over in her mind. *THIS WAS NEVER YOURS.* The words had weight. Not anger — certainty. As though the writer believed it so completely they didn't need to argue.

Tom dozed in the chair opposite her, boots still on, posture deceptively relaxed. She knew better. He was the kind of man who rested without ever fully letting go of awareness. The kind who would hear the wrong sound through stone and wake already moving.

Near dawn, the bush shifted again.

This time, Alice heard it before she saw it — the uneasy silence of animals pulling back. No insects. No distant rustle. Just the creek and her own breath.

She sat up slowly.

"Tom," she whispered.

His eyes opened immediately.

"What?"

"Listen."

They stayed still, the house holding its breath with them. Then came the sound — faint, careful, unmistakable.

Footsteps.

Not on the verandah. Not near the doors.

Out back. Near the creek track.

Tom rose without a word and eased toward the kitchen window. Alice followed, keeping to his shadow. He nudged the curtain aside just enough to see.

A figure moved between the trees.

Not rushing. Not hiding.

Walking the track like it belonged to them.

Tom's jaw set. "He's pushing."

"He wants me to react," Alice whispered.

"Yes."

She inhaled slowly. "Then I won't."

Tom glanced at her, surprise flickering across his face. "You sure?"

She nodded. "He thinks fear will make me run. Or fight badly. I'm not giving him either."

The figure paused near the creek bend, just long enough to look toward the house. Even at this distance, Alice felt the weight of the stare.

Then the person turned and disappeared back into the trees.

The light crept into the sky not long after, softening the world again. Day made things look manageable. It always had.

They sat at the kitchen table with mugs of tea they barely touched.

"He'll escalate," Tom said finally.

"Yes," Alice agreed. "But not yet."

He studied her. "You've changed."

She met his gaze. "So have you."

A knock came at the front door — firm, official.

Alice jumped.

Tom reached it first, opening the door to reveal Senior Constable Helen Price, hat in hand, expression unreadable. A Taravale local, born and bred. Someone who knew exactly where every family sat in the town's unspoken hierarchy.

"Morning," Helen said. "Mind if I come in?"

Alice joined them in the hallway. "Of course."

Helen stepped inside, eyes flicking once — just once — down the corridor toward the closed door, then back to Alice.

"Had a report last night," she said. "Anonymous. About trespassing."

Alice's mouth tightened. "On whose property?"

Helen didn't hesitate. "Yours."

Tom's shoulders tensed. "Funny way to report your own behaviour."

Helen's gaze flicked to him. "Funny town."

She turned back to Alice. "Anyone bother you?"

Alice considered the question carefully. "Someone left a message."

Helen raised an eyebrow. "Did they."

Alice nodded once. "Yes."

"And?"

"And I don't intend to be intimidated."

A beat passed.

Helen exhaled slowly, like someone choosing a path. "All right," she said. "Then here's what I can do — and what I can't."

She lowered her voice. "Officially, there's not much. No forced entry. No damage. No witnesses willing to put their name to anything."

Tom scoffed. Helen ignored him.

"Unofficially," she continued, "I can keep an eye on things. And I can advise you to document everything."

Alice gestured toward the kitchen. "Already started."

Helen's gaze sharpened. "Good."

She paused at the door on her way out. "Be careful, Alice. This isn't about land anymore. It's about pride."

After she left, the house felt different again — less isolated, but more exposed.

Alice stared at the closed door at the end of the hallway.

"He's trying to get ahead of it," she said.

Tom nodded. "Which means we're closer than he likes."

She took a breath, steadying herself. "Then we keep going."

Tom looked at her like he always had when she set her mind to something — with concern, admiration, and the quiet acceptance that stopping her was pointless.

Outside, Taravale woke fully.

And somewhere in the bush, a man who had always believed the land belonged to him was realising that silence no longer protected him.

# CHAPTER TWELVE

Helen Price's visit lingered in the house long after her car disappeared down the track.

Not as reassurance. As proof.

Proof that this wasn't imagination or nerves or a house full of echoes. Proof that whatever line had been crossed last night had been noticed - and quietly acknowledged - by people who preferred lines to stay where they were.

Alice gathered the papers from the chest and spread them across the kitchen table again, this time without ceremony. Daylight stripped them of their mystery but not their meaning. Ink was still ink. Lines were still lines.

Tom leaned over her shoulder, careful not to crowd her. "The creek boundary here," he said, tapping the map lightly, "never matched the fence. Everyone just... stopped questioning it."

"Because questioning would have meant admitting it was wrong," Alice replied.

"And that would've cost people more than money."

She traced the creek line again, following it to the circled section. "This is where the track comes through. Where the gate was."

Tom nodded. "Where he's been entering."

Alice looked up. "So he knows this part isn't his."

"He knows it *might not be*," Tom corrected. "Which is worse."

They worked quietly for a while after that. Alice photographed each page again, backing them up twice this time. Tom made notes - dates, names, references to fencing works and water rights that hadn't meant much to him until now.

By mid-morning, the house had warmed enough to feel almost benign. Birds returned to the trees. A breeze lifted the curtains in the kitchen window.

It would have been easy to believe the worst was over.

"I need to go into town," Alice said eventually.

Tom looked up sharply. "Now?"

"Yes." She met his gaze. "If he's watching, I want him to see I'm not hiding."

"That cuts both ways."

"I know."

Tom considered, then nodded. "I'll come."

"No," she said gently. "Not this time."

His jaw tightened. "Alice—"

"If we arrive together, it's a statement," she said. "I don't want that yet. I want normal."

He held her gaze for a long moment, then sighed. "I don't like it."

"You never did."

A ghost of a smile flickered across his mouth. "Call me when you get there."

She nodded and grabbed her keys.

The drive into Taravale felt different now. Not hostile. Watchful.

She parked near the general store and post office, the heart of the town beating quietly around her. Jo Reid stood behind the counter, sorting mail with brisk efficiency.

She looked up as Alice entered.

"Well," Jo said. "You've brought a bit of excitement back with you."

Alice kept her expression neutral. "So I've heard."

Jo slid a parcel across the counter and lowered her voice. "You be careful up there."

"Why?" Alice asked.

Jo's mouth thinned. "Because some people don't like being reminded the past still exists."

Alice nodded. "Thank you."

Outside, she crossed to Mara's coffee van. Mara handed her a cup without being asked.

"On the house," she said. "Looks like you could use it."

Alice wrapped her hands around the warmth. "Everyone's very kind today."

Mara's gaze flicked down the street. "Everyone's very curious."

"Has he said anything?"

Mara shook her head. "Not directly. But he's been... restless."

Alice took a sip. "Good."

Mara smiled slightly. "That's one word for it."

Alice stayed long enough to be seen - to exchange greetings, to buy bread, to exist - then drove back toward the farmhouse with a steadiness that surprised her.

When she reached the gate, she stopped.

The latch was open.

Not wide. Not dramatic.

Just unhooked.

Alice didn't get out of the ute straight away. She sat there with her hands on the wheel, the engine ticking softly, and felt something settle into place inside her.

Fear, yes.

But beneath it, something harder.

Resolve.

She got out, latched the gate firmly, and drove up to the house.

Inside, the house waited - cool stone, light-filled rooms, dark corners holding their breath.

Alice set her bag down and went straight to the closed room. She opened the chest and lifted out the papers again, this time without hesitation.

If Gavin Millson wanted silence, he'd chosen the wrong woman to scare.

And if Taravale wanted things left buried, it should have stopped pretending the land forgot.

Outside, the creek kept running.

And somewhere beyond the trees, someone realised that watching was no longer enough.

# CHAPTER THIRTEEN

The phone rang just after Alice finished scanning the last document.

Not her mobile - the landline.

The sound startled her anyway. A sharp, old-fashioned ring that cut through the quiet like it had been waiting years to be used. She stared at it from the kitchen bench, pulse skidding, half-expecting it to stop before she touched it.

It didn't.

She lifted the receiver. "Hello?"

Silence answered.

Not dead- line silence - breathing silence. The faint hiss of a connection held open on purpose.

Alice straightened. "You've reached the Gordon place," she said evenly. "If you're calling to trespass, you're too late."

A breath. Slow. Controlled.

Then a voice she didn't recognise, pitched lower than Gavin's, rougher at the edges.

"You don't know what you're holding."

Her grip tightened on the receiver. "I know exactly what I'm holding."

A pause. She could almost hear the recalculation.

"That land was never meant to be divided the way it was," the voice said. "Your grandfather understood that."

"He understood theft," Alice replied. "And he documented it."

A sharp exhale. "You think paper changes what people believe belongs to them?"

"Yes," she said. "Eventually."

The line went dead.

Alice replaced the receiver carefully, like any sudden movement might splinter her resolve. Her reflection stared back at her from the darkened window - eyes bright, jaw set, someone she was only just meeting properly.

She didn't sit down.

She went straight to the hallway and opened the closed door again.

This time, the room didn't feel heavy. It felt expectant.

She pulled the chest out fully and began sorting the papers properly - grouping letters, receipts, maps. Patterns emerged quickly once she stopped skimming. Dates clustered. Names repeated. Payments recorded where they shouldn't have been. Fence repairs funded by people who didn't own the land they were fixing.

One name appeared again and again alongside the Millsons.

Not Gavin.

His father.

The house creaked softly behind her as if acknowledging the shift.

Her phone buzzed on the kitchen table.

**Tom:** You back?

She typed quickly.

**Alice:** Yes. Someone just called the landline.

The reply came almost immediately.

**Tom:** I'm coming.

She didn't argue this time.

By the time Tom arrived, dusk had begun its slow descent again. He read the documents in silence, his expression darkening with each page.

"This isn't just boundary creep," he said finally. "This is systematic."

"Yes," Alice said. "And it didn't stop with my grandfather."

Tom looked up sharply. "What do you mean?"

She slid one of the letters toward him. "These payments continue for years after he died. Same handwriting. Same account."

Tom's jaw tightened. "Someone kept it going."

"And someone benefited."

They fell quiet again.

Outside, the bush shifted - not the nervous hush of the night before, but the restless movement of animals unsettled by change. The creek sounded louder, swollen by something upstream.

Tom closed the folder carefully. "You've crossed the point of no return."

Alice nodded. "I know."

He studied her face. "Are you scared?"

She considered the question honestly. "Yes."

"Good," he said. "Means you're paying attention."

A sound echoed faintly from outside.

Metal.

A gate.

Not the front this time.

The creek track.

Tom was already moving. Alice followed, heart hammering, stopping just inside the doorway as he stepped onto the verandah and swept the torch beam across the yard.

The beam caught movement near the trees - a shape retreating, fast and angry now, no longer careful.

And something else.

A fresh spray of white paint across the stone wall beneath the sitting room window.

Tom swore softly.

Alice stepped forward and read the words aloud, her voice steady despite the chill racing through her veins.

**STOP DIGGING.**

She looked at Tom, something fierce and unyielding settling into her bones.

"They're running out of ways to ask nicely," she said.

Tom nodded. "Which means the truth's closer than it's ever been."

The paint gleamed wetly in the torchlight, a mark meant to intimidate.

Instead, it felt like confirmation.

Because people only try to silence you when you're finally saying something that matters.

# CHAPTER FOURTEEN

The paint was still wet.

Alice could smell it - sharp and chemical, cutting through the familiar scents of stone and damp earth. It sat wrong against the house, too modern, too loud. The words beneath the sitting room window looked almost obscene, as if someone had scrawled graffiti across a gravestone.

Tom crouched, running the torch beam slowly over the stone. "They didn't rush this," he said. "They wanted it legible. Wanted you to see it in daylight."

"They wanted me to wake up to it," Alice replied.

"Yes."

She folded her arms, the night air suddenly colder against her skin. "Can it be removed?"

"Eventually." He straightened. "But not tonight."

She met his gaze. "Good. I don't want it gone yet."

Tom studied her, a flicker of something unreadable passing through his eyes. "You're sure?"

"Yes." She looked back at the words. *STOP DIGGING.* "If I clean it off now, it becomes something that almost happened. I want it to stay long enough to be seen."

"By who?"

"By anyone who drives past. By anyone who thinks this is just a paperwork dispute."

He nodded slowly. "You've thought this through."

"Not consciously," she said. "But I'm done pretending this is small."

They went back inside and locked the doors again, Tom checking the windows while Alice rinsed her hands at the sink, scrubbing away the phantom smell of paint. Her reflection in the glass looked steadier than she felt, but there was something else there now too - resolve sharpened into something harder.

"Sit," Tom said gently, guiding her toward the table.

She did, wrapping her hands around the mug he slid toward her. The tea had gone cold. She didn't care.

"Tomorrow," he said, "we take this beyond Taravale."

Alice's gaze snapped up. "How?"

"You don't win against people like this by staying quiet and local," he replied. "You widen the circle."

She nodded slowly. "Surveyor?"

"Yes. Independent. And a solicitor who isn't from here."

"That will make things worse."

Tom's mouth curved into a grim half-smile. "Eventually. Which means first it'll make things loud."

Alice let out a breath she hadn't realised she was holding. "He'll blame me for that."

"He already does."

A soft knock sounded at the door.

Both of them froze.

Tom moved first, hand lifted in a silent instruction for her to stay back. He approached the door carefully and opened it just enough to see through the gap.

Mara stood on the verandah, wrapped in a jacket too thin for the night, eyes sharp despite the hour.

"I saw the paint," she said quietly. "Thought you might need another witness."

Tom opened the door fully and stepped aside. "Come in."

Mara crossed the threshold and stopped short when she saw the words through the sitting room window. Her jaw tightened.

"Well," she said softly. "That's bold."

"That's desperation," Alice corrected.

Mara glanced at her, a spark of approval in her eyes. "You're not wrong."

She moved closer to the window, studying the message. "This changes things."

"Yes," Alice said. "It makes them accountable."

Mara nodded once. "Then here's what happens next. People will talk. Gavin will deny. Someone else will quietly try to smooth it over." Her gaze flicked back to Alice. "Don't let them."

"I won't."

Mara smiled - small, fierce. "Good. Because this town has needed someone like you for a long time."

She headed for the door, then paused. "I'll tell Helen in the morning. Officially."

Tom inclined his head. "Thank you."

After Mara left, the house felt fuller somehow - less isolated, less easily claimed by the dark.

Alice stood at the window, staring at the words on the stone wall. "They think they're warning me," she said. "But all they've done is prove it matters."

Tom came to stand beside her, close enough that she could feel his warmth without being crowded.

"You're not alone in this," he said quietly.

She leaned into him, just slightly. Not seeking comfort so much as acknowledging it.

Outside, the creek surged louder, fed by something unseen upstream.

The land was shifting.

And for the first time since she'd returned, Alice felt certain of one thing:

Whatever Taravale had buried, it was ready to come back to the surface.

# CHAPTER FIFTEEN

The storm arrived before dawn.

Alice woke to the sound of it gathering - not rain yet, but the low, distant movement of air through the trees, a pressure change that settled deep in her chest. The fire had long since burned out. The house felt colder, tighter, as if bracing itself.

Tom was already awake.

She knew without opening her eyes. His presence had a way of shifting the space around it, of sharpening the quiet. When she did open them, she found him standing at the window, watching the sky lighten to a bruised grey.

"Creek'll rise," he said quietly.

"How fast?"

"Fast enough to matter."

The first crack of thunder rolled across the valley moments later, followed by rain - sudden and heavy, drumming against the roof like it had been waiting its turn. The gutters overflowed almost immediately. Water tracked down the stone walls, darkening them until the house looked older somehow, more exposed.

Alice sat up, heart thudding. "If the creek floods—"

"The track'll go first," Tom finished. "Then the low paddock."

"And the boundary."

"Yes."

The word hung between them.

They moved quickly then, pulling on boots, jackets, gathering torches and phones, checking doors. Tom opened the back door and stepped onto the verandah, rain soaking him instantly. Alice followed, the smell of wet earth rising sharp and clean.

The yard was already slick. Water pooled where dust had been the day before. The gumtrees swayed, shedding bark and leaves that plastered themselves to the ground.

Tom pointed toward the creek line. "You see it?"

She squinted through the rain. The creek had widened, the gentle ribbon now a dark, churning band, water spilling into places it didn't usually reach.

Something pale bobbed near the edge.

Alice's breath caught. "Is that—"

"A fence post," Tom said grimly. "One of the old ones."

They stood there as the storm intensified, thunder cracking close enough to rattle the windows. The house groaned, settling into its foundations like it always had when weather tested it.

Alice pulled her phone from her pocket.

No signal.

She checked anyway. Still nothing.

The landline rang.

They looked at each other.

Tom reached it first, lifting the receiver. "Yes?"

A voice crackled through the line, distorted by static and rain. Helen Price.

"Road's cut," she said without preamble. "Creek's over already. You two all right up there?"

"We're fine," Tom replied. "For now."

A pause. "I've got Gavin on the other line. He's reporting concerns about flood damage to *his* boundary fence."

Alice let out a short, humourless laugh.

Tom's jaw tightened. "Tell him to stay off the track."

"I did," Helen said. "Didn't sound pleased."

The line went dead.

Outside, the rain shifted, driven sideways now, the storm fully upon them. Alice watched the water claim more ground, erase the neatness of boundaries and tracks alike.

"This isn't coincidence," she said.

"No," Tom agreed. "This is what he's afraid of."

The creek surged again, swallowing the last visible marker between properties. Fence, post, wire - all gone beneath the water.

For a moment, everything blurred into one moving, unstoppable force.

The land didn't care who claimed it.

It remembered its own shape.

Alice felt something settle inside her then - not fear, not triumph, but clarity.

"When the water drops," she said, "there won't be anything left to argue with."

Tom looked at her, rain dripping from his hair, eyes steady. "That's when it gets dangerous."

Thunder split the sky overhead, close enough to make her flinch. The house held.

The storm raged on, remapping the land in real time.

And somewhere out there, a man who'd relied on fixed lines and quiet intimidation was watching them wash away, realising too late that nature was not on his side.

Nor was Alice Gordon.

# CHAPTER SIXTEEN

The storm broke as abruptly as it had arrived.

Rain eased from a roar to a steady insistence, then to a fine mist that hung in the air like breath. The creek still ran high, dark and swollen, but its anger had dulled into momentum. Water slid back into itself, reluctant but obedient.

Alice and Tom stood on the verandah long after the worst had passed, watching the land re- emerge.

Debris lay everywhere - branches, bark, fence wire twisted into unfamiliar shapes. The track to the creek had vanished completely, erased beneath mud and waterlogged grass. Where the boundary fence had once drawn its neat, arguable line, there was now only churned earth and pooled water.

"No fence," Alice said quietly.

Tom shook his head. "Not anymore."

She hugged her jacket closer, the cold finally finding its way in. "That means he can't pretend the line still exists."

"It also means he'll try to put one back," Tom replied. "Fast."

"Before anyone official sees it."

"Yes."

They moved carefully down the steps, boots sinking into mud. Tom tested the ground ahead with each step, reading it the way he always had - pressure, resistance, slope. Alice followed his lead, eyes scanning for anything that didn't belong.

Near the creek's edge, something dark lay half-buried in silt.

Tom crouched and pulled it free.

A length of old fencing wire. Not rusted. Newer. Cut cleanly at one end.

Alice's chest tightened. "He was already planning to reinforce it."

Tom nodded. "Or move it."

She looked out over the flattened ground. "The land beat him to it."

They didn't speak again until they were back inside, stripping off wet jackets and boots by the door. The house felt different now - not calmer, exactly, but more settled, like it had released something it had been holding through the storm.

Alice poured hot water over tea leaves and handed Tom a mug. "Helen will want to see this."

"Yes," he said. "And a surveyor will need to come while the evidence is fresh."

She sat at the table, exhaustion finally catching up to her. "He won't wait."

Tom leaned against the bench. "No. He'll act."

As if summoned by the thought, the sound of an engine drifted through the open window - distant but purposeful.

Alice stiffened. "That's him."

Tom moved to the window and looked out toward the track. "He's not supposed to be here."

The ute appeared between the trees, tyres throwing mud, moving faster than conditions allowed. It stopped short of the washed- out section, brake lights flaring.

Gavin climbed out.

Even from this distance, Alice could see the tension in his posture, the way he surveyed the land as if it had personally betrayed him. He took a few steps forward, then stopped, staring at the absence where the fence should have been.

Tom exhaled slowly. "This is where it turns."

Alice stood and joined him at the window. "What do we do?"

"We document," Tom said. "And we don't engage unless we have to."

Outside, Gavin pulled his phone from his pocket, pacing, gesturing sharply toward the creek. He kicked at the mud in frustration, then bent and grabbed a fallen post, hauling it upright as if sheer will could make it matter again.

"He's going to try to reset it," Alice said.

"Not legally," Tom replied. "And not without witnesses."

As if on cue, another vehicle appeared on the track behind Gavin's ute.

Mara's coffee van.

It pulled up well back from the creek, hazard lights flashing. Mara climbed out, arms folded, eyes sharp. She didn't approach - just stood where she was, watching.

Alice felt a strange, fierce gratitude.

Gavin noticed her then. His head snapped around, gaze lifting toward the house. Even at this distance, Alice felt the weight of it - anger stripped of civility now, bare and exposed.

He took a step toward the house.

Tom's hand settled lightly at the small of her back, grounding. "Stay."

Gavin stopped again, visibly recalculating. He looked back at Mara. At the van. At the land that no longer obeyed him.

Finally, he turned away.

He climbed back into his ute and drove off, tyres slipping in the mud, retreating the way people did when they knew they'd lost the ground they stood on.

Alice sagged slightly. "That's not over."

"No," Tom agreed. "But it's changed."

She nodded, eyes still on the place where the fence had been. "So have I."

Inside, the house creaked softly, settling into its altered landscape.

Outside, the creek continued to run - not as a threat now, but as a reminder.

The land had spoken.

And for the first time, it had been heard.

# CHAPTER SEVENTEEN

The quiet after Gavin left was heavier than the storm.

It settled over the house in layers - mud-scented air, damp timber, stone that still held cold in its bones. Alice stood at the window long after his ute disappeared, watching the land as if it might rearrange itself again now that no one was looking.

Tom didn't rush her.

He moved around the kitchen instead, making space for normal things to exist. He wiped mud from the floor, hung jackets where they could dry, stacked firewood closer to the hearth. The small, practical acts grounded the room, tethered it to something human.

"Come sit," he said eventually.

She didn't argue. She sank into the chair opposite him at the table, fatigue pressing down hard now that adrenaline had nothing left to feed on. Her hands shook slightly when she wrapped them around the mug.

"He was going to move the fence," she said.

"Yes."

"He would've done it today."

"Yes."

"And if the storm hadn't come—"

Tom met her gaze. "Then we'd be arguing about lines drawn by men who benefited from them."

She swallowed. "Instead we're arguing with water."

"Water doesn't lie," he said. "It just takes what it needs."

The house creaked faintly, a sound Alice was beginning to understand rather than fear.

She looked down at the table, at the papers she'd stacked neatly beside her mug. "There's more," she said quietly. "I didn't show you everything."

Tom didn't react - not outwardly. "What kind of more?"

She slid a letter toward him. "This one wasn't in the chest. It was behind it. Tucked into the lining."

He read it slowly, once, then again. His jaw tightened.

"It's a confession," he said.

"Yes."

"To what?"

"To knowing the fence was wrong. To letting it stay that way because pushing back would have meant trouble." Her voice wavered, then steadied. "My grandfather didn't start it. But he didn't stop it either."

Tom leaned back, exhaling slowly. "That's not thc samc thing."

"It feels close enough."

He met her eyes. "People make choices with the tools they have. Silence is one of them."

Alice pressed her lips together. "Silence is expensive."

"Yes," he agreed. "And someone always pays."

The truth of it settled heavily between them.

Outside, the creek's voice had lowered again, but it was still louder than it had been before. The land had shifted. It would take time to look the same, if it ever did.

Alice pushed the letter back into the stack. "Helen needs to see all of this."

"She will," Tom said. "And so will a solicitor."

"And the town?"

He hesitated. "Eventually."

She nodded, bracing herself. "That's when the stories start."

"Already have," he said gently. "You just weren't here to hear them before."

A knock sounded at the door.

Not sharp. Not demanding.

Measured.

Tom stood, his movements calm. He opened the door to find Helen Price standing on the verandah, rain jacket still on, boots caked in mud.

"Thought I'd catch you before things got... interpreted," she said.

Alice joined them in the hallway. "You saw him."

Helen nodded. "I did. And I saw him leave."

She stepped inside, eyes taking in the room, the papers on the table, the quiet determination settling into the space.

"You weren't imagining things," Helen said to Alice. "And you weren't wrong to document."

Alice let out a breath she'd been holding since dawn.

Helen continued, lowering her voice. "Gavin's already made calls. Claimed flood damage. Claimed provocation."

"Provocation?" Alice echoed.

Helen's mouth twitched without humour. "You existing, mostly."

Tom folded his arms. "What happens now?"

Helen considered. "Now it becomes official. Surveyor. Temporary injunction if he tries to rebuild the fence. And a reminder to certain people that intimidation is still a crime, even when it's polite."

Alice met her gaze. "Will it stick?"

Helen's eyes were steady. "If you keep doing exactly what you're doing."

When she left, the house felt quieter again - but not alone.

Alice sank back into her chair, the exhaustion finally breaking through. "I didn't expect this," she said softly. "Any of it."

Tom watched her for a long moment. "You came back anyway."

She gave a tired smile. "Seems I can't help myself."

He reached across the table then, covering her hand with his. It was a simple thing. Grounded. Real.

"Stay," he said quietly. Not a demand. Not even a request.

A truth.

Alice looked at their joined hands, at the papers beside them, at the house that had held all of it without flinching.

"I am," she said.

Outside, the land lay scarred but honest.

Inside, something long buried had finally been spoken aloud.

And Taravale, whether it liked it or not, would have to learn how to live with that.

# CHAPTER EIGHTEEN

News travelled faster than the water had.

By midday, Taravale knew there had been trouble at the old Gordon place - not the details, not yet, but the shape of it. Trouble with history. Trouble with land. The kind that didn't stay neatly contained once it surfaced.

Alice felt it in the way people looked at her when she drove back into town with Tom that afternoon. Not hostile. Not welcoming either. Curious, cautious - mcasuring whcrc shc now sat in the town's quiet hierarchy.

They parked outside the pub.

"Why here?" Alice asked as Tom cut the engine.

"Because this is where stories get corrected," he said. "Or made worse."

Inside, the air was cool and dim, the scent of old timber and beer grounding in its familiarity. Bill

Kershaw stood behind the bar, polishing a glass he'd already polished twice.

He looked up as they entered.

"Well," he said mildly. "Was wondering when you'd show."

Alice met his gaze. "You already know."

Bill snorted. "I know a storm took out a fence that shouldn't have been where it was. Everything else is commentary."

Tom leaned a forearm on the bar. "Who's talking?"

"Everyone," Bill replied. "But not loudly."

Alice slid onto a stool. "What version are they telling?"

Bill considered. "That you've come back to sell. That Gavin's worried about access. That the creek's always been unpredictable." He met her eyes. "And that some people are nervous."

"About what?"

"About what happens when the wrong person stops being quiet."

The truth of it settled in her chest.

A man at the far end of the bar stood and left without finishing his drink. Another glanced their way, then looked down at his phone.

Bill set two glasses on the bar and filled them without asking. "You didn't start this," he said quietly. "But you might finish it."

Alice wrapped her fingers around the glass. "I don't want to hurt the town."

Bill's mouth twitched. "Town's been hurting itself for years."

The door opened again.

Gavin Millson walked in.

The conversation inside dropped by half - not silence, but a thinning, as if the room had collectively inhaled and wasn't sure when to exhale again.

He spotted Alice immediately.

His smile was careful. "Alice. Thought that might be you."

She didn't smile back. "Gavin."

Tom didn't move.

Gavin approached the bar, positioning himself close enough to be heard without raising his voice. "I hear there's been some... confusion."

"About ownership?" Alice asked.

"About intent," Gavin corrected. "You coming back stirred things. People get defensive."

"People who benefit from lies do," Tom said flatly.

Gavin's eyes flicked to him. "This isn't your fight."

"It is when intimidation starts," Tom replied.

Bill cleared his throat. "You want a drink, Gavin, or just an audience?"

Gavin ignored him, gaze fixed on Alice. "You don't have to push this. There are ways to resolve it quietly."

Alice leaned forward, meeting his eyes. "Quietly for who?"

A flicker of irritation broke through his calm. "You don't understand the consequences."

"I understand them perfectly," she said. "I've been living with them since I was a child."

The room held its breath.

Gavin straightened. "If you keep digging, you'll find more than you want."

Alice didn't look away. "That's the point."

For a moment, something like naked calculation crossed his face. Then the smile returned - thinner now.

"We'll see," he said, and turned away.

He left without ordering a drink.

Only when the door closed did the room begin to breathe again.

Tom drained his glass. "He's cornered."

Alice nodded. "And cornered people don't stay polite."

Outside, the afternoon sun burned away the last of the storm's heaviness. The creek still ran high, but it no longer threatened.

Alice stepped out onto the footpath and looked down Taravale's main street - the pub, the general store, the coffee van parked a little way off like a quiet sentinel.

She felt it then.

Not fear.

Belonging.

Not the easy kind - the earned kind.

Whatever came next, this wasn't just her fight anymore.

And Taravale had just chosen to watch it unfold.

# CHAPTER NINETEEN

The first stone came through the sitting room window just after midnight.

Alice was awake when it happened - not alert exactly, but not asleep either. The kind of half-rest that came from days spent holding tension like a second spine. The crash shattered the quiet, glass exploding inward with a violence that felt personal.

She was on her feet before the sound finished echoing.

"Tom!"

He was already moving, pulling her back from the doorway as another stone struck the outer wall, hard enough to thud through stone and timber.

"Down," he said, firm and low.

They crouched behind the kitchen bench as glass tinkled onto the floor behind them. The fire crackled, absurdly calm. Outside, footsteps pounded across the yard - not careful now, not watching.

Running.

Tom reached for the torch and flicked it on, angling the beam low. "Stay here."

"No," Alice said immediately.

He met her eyes. "I need you safe."

"I need to see."

They moved together to the kitchen window, staying below the sill. Tom lifted the torch just enough to catch movement near the trees - a shape retreating fast, shoulders hunched, no attempt to hide now.

"Was it him?" Alice whispered.

"No," Tom said. "Too young. Too quick."

A hired message.

They waited until the night swallowed the movement completely before standing. Tom crossed to the sitting room carefully, scanning the ground as he went. Alice followed despite herself, heart hammering.

The window was gone.

Shards littered the floor, glittering like ice. The chair sat exactly where it had been earlier, sheet half-slid from the back - as if whoever threw the stone had aimed deliberately.

There was something else on the floor.

Alice bent and picked it up.

A length of fencing wire, twisted into a crude loop.

Her stomach dropped.

"He's not hiding anymore," she said.

"No," Tom agreed. "He's outsourcing."

Alice's phone buzzed in her hand.

A message. Unknown number.

**You were warned.**

She stared at the screen until the words blurred.

Tom took the phone gently from her hand and set it face down on the table. "This changes things."

"Yes," she said. Her voice didn't shake. "It makes it criminal."

He nodded. "And public."

They didn't clean up the glass.

Not yet.

Tom called Helen. She arrived within the hour, lights off as she pulled into the drive, face set hard as she surveyed the damage.

"This," she said quietly, "is no longer a disagreement."

She photographed everything - the window, the wire, the footprints already fading in the dirt.

Alice stood beside her, watching the house absorb yet another mark of intrusion.

Helen straightened and met her gaze. "If you were thinking of backing off, now's the time to decide."

Alice didn't hesitate. "I'm not."

Helen nodded. "Good. Because neither am I."

When the patrol car finally left, dawn was already bruising the horizon.

Tom swept glass into a bucket while Alice taped plastic over the broken window. The house looked wounded now.

As the first light crept across the stone walls, Alice stood back and took it in.

"They're trying to make this unbearable," she said.

Tom set the broom aside. "They've misjudged you."

She looked at him then - really looked. The steadiness. The quiet fury held in check. The way he stayed.

"I'm not leaving," she said again, but this time it wasn't a promise. It was a fact.

Outside, Taravale began to wake.

And somewhere nearby, someone who had relied on silence and distance had crossed a line they couldn't uncross.

The land had kept its secrets long enough.

Now it was demanding the truth.

# CHAPTER TWENTY

By morning, the house looked like a crime scene.

Not because it was cordoned off - Taravale didn't do spectacle - but because everything felt examined. Measured. Marked. Helen's boot prints still dented the mud near the sitting room window. The plastic over the broken glass fluttered faintly in the breeze, snapping once in a way that made Alice flinch despite herself.

Tom noticed. He always did.

"It'll settle," he said quietly, handing her a mug. "The noise is worse right after."

Alice nodded and wrapped her hands around the warmth. Sleep had never come back after the stone. Adrenaline had burned it off, leaving her hollowed out and sharp-edged all at once.

Helen returned mid-morning with a uniformed constable Alice didn't recognise - younger, careful, eyes taking everything in without judgement.

"We'll log it properly," Helen said. "Statement, photos, chain of custody for the wire."

Alice watched the younger constable bag the twisted fencing wire like it was something fragile. "You think he'll deny it?"

Helen's mouth flattened. "He'll deny ordering it. Not the intent."

"And the number that messaged me?"

"We'll trace it. Burner or not, people always get sloppy."

Alice believed her. Or wanted to.

After they left, the house felt quieter again - not safe, exactly, but steadied by the sense that something had shifted from private to public. That mattered.

Tom stood at the kitchen window, watching the track. "He won't come himself now."

"Because it's documented."

"Yes." He turned to her. "But he'll push in other ways."

Alice took a breath. "Then we keep pushing back."

The surveyor arrived just after lunch.

Independent. From two towns over. A man with sun-weathered skin and a calm, methodical way of moving. He walked the flooded boundary with Tom, measuring, marking, taking photos of the creek's natural line now laid bare.

"This," he said eventually, gesturing to the water's edge, "is the true boundary. Always has been."

Alice felt something loosen in her chest she hadn't realised she'd been holding for years.

"And the fence?" she asked.

"Never should've been there," he replied. "Storm just corrected it."

Tom's mouth twitched. "The land has opinions."

The surveyor smiled faintly. "It usually wins."

By late afternoon, word had spread properly.

Mara stopped by with coffee and updates she pretended weren't updates. Bill rang to say the pub was buzzing. Jo at the store had quietly set aside copies of old rate notices "just in case".

The town was choosing sides - not loudly, not yet - but visibly.

Alice stood in the sitting room as the light shifted toward evening, the plastic still rippling over the broken window. She reached up and touched the stone beneath the painted words outside, now partially washed by rain.

"They wanted to scare me," she said.

Tom came to stand beside her. "They wanted you gone."

She shook her head. "They wanted me small."

He looked at her then, something unmistakably proud in his eyes. "They've failed."

Outside, the creek kept running - no longer a threat, no longer a secret. Just water following the shape it had always known.

Alice turned back to the table where the papers lay, neatly stacked, no longer hidden. "What happens now?"

Tom didn't hesitate. "Now we finish it."

She nodded once.

The land had spoken.

The town was listening.

And for the first time since she'd returned, Alice knew exactly where she stood - not just on a map, but in the story Taravale was finally being forced to tell.

# CHAPTER TWENTY-ONE

The night came in quietly.

No storm this time. No drama. Just the slow settling of dark across paddocks and creek, the land easing into itself as if it had said everything it needed to say for now. That unsettled Alice more than the noise ever had.

Silence meant thinking.

She sat at the kitchen table with the papers spread out once more, not reading them so much as tracing them — dates, margins, the pressure of pen strokes. Her grandfather's hand. Then another, later, mimicking it just enough to pass without scrutiny.

Tom watched from the doorway, arms folded, a mug cooling in his hands.

"You've found something," he said.

She didn't look up. "Not something new. Something connected."

He crossed the room and leaned over her shoulder. "Show me."

Alice tapped one receipt, then another, then a third. "Fence repairs. Paid from different accounts. Years apart." She slid a letter beside them. "Same phrasing. Same justification. 'Temporary adjustment.'"

Tom's jaw tightened. "Temporary things don't last forty years."

"No," she said. "But lies do."

She pushed back from the table and stood, pacing once before stopping dead. "It wasn't just Gavin's father. It was a group."

Tom straightened. "Who?"

"Men who sat on boards. Committees. Councils." Her voice hardened. "Men who decided it was easier to keep quiet than challenge the Millsons."

"And your grandfather?"

"He tried to document it," she said softly. "Then he stopped."

Tom met her eyes. "Because he was told to."

She nodded. "Or because he realised no one would back him."

The house creaked, a slow, familiar sound that no longer startled her. It felt like agreement.

Tom exhaled slowly. "If this goes to court—"

"It will," Alice said.

"It will tear the town apart."

She looked out the window toward the dark line of gums. "The town's already torn. This just makes the seams visible."

A sound drifted in from outside — an engine, distant but deliberate. Not fast. Not hiding.

Tom moved to the window, tension sharpening his posture. "Someone's coming up the track."

Alice joined him. Headlights crept between the trees, pausing briefly near the creek before continuing toward the house.

Her pulse steadied instead of spiking.

"That's Gavin," she said.

The ute stopped short of the verandah. The engine cut. For a moment, nothing happened.

Then a door slammed.

Footsteps approached — slower than before, heavier. No attempt at stealth. This was no message thrown from the dark.

This was a confrontation.

Tom reached for the torch, but Alice caught his wrist. "No. Let him."

He searched her face. "Alice—"

"I need to hear it."

The knock came — firm, deliberate, three solid raps.

Alice walked to the door before Tom could stop her. She opened it and stepped onto the verandah.

Gavin Millson stood there alone.

No smile this time. No civility. His jacket was unbuttoned, his hair damp with sweat despite the cool night. His eyes flicked past her into the house, then back again.

"You've made your point," he said.

Alice folded her arms. "Have I?"

"You're dragging the town into something it doesn't need."

She tilted her head slightly. "You dragged the town into it decades ago."

His mouth tightened. "You don't know the full story."

"Then tell it," she said. "All of it."

Silence stretched between them, thick and loaded.

Finally, Gavin exhaled. "That land was going to be lost. Subdivided. Sold off. My father—" He stopped, jaw working. "He believed keeping it together mattered more than paperwork."

Alice's voice was calm. "So he stole it."

Gavin's eyes flashed. "He protected it."

"For himself," Tom said from behind her.

Gavin's gaze flicked to him. "You always were self-righteous."

Tom didn't rise to it. "You crossed a line."

Gavin looked back at Alice, something like desperation creeping in around the edges. "This doesn't end well for you."

Alice met his stare without blinking. "It already has."

He laughed then — short, brittle. "You think you've won?"

"No," she said. "I think I've stopped losing."

The words landed harder than any accusation.

For a moment, it looked like Gavin might say more. Confess. Threaten. Beg.

Instead, he stepped back.

"You're making enemies," he said quietly.

Alice nodded. "I know."

Gavin turned and walked back down the verandah steps. His ute started moments later, headlights flaring as he reversed, then disappeared back down the track.

The night closed in again.

Tom stepped beside her, close enough that their shoulders touched. "You didn't flinch."

She exhaled slowly. "Neither did the land."

They went back inside and locked the door.

Behind them, the house settled — stone and timber holding firm.

And somewhere in the dark, a man who had always believed power lived in silence finally understood that he'd lost control of the story.

# CHAPTER TWENTY-TWO

Alice slept for exactly two hours.

She knew because she checked the clock when she woke - 2:14 a.m. - and because her body felt like it had been dropped back into itself too abruptly, every nerve lit and listening. The house was quiet in the way that didn't invite rest. Not waiting. Holding.

She lay still and catalogued sounds.

Creek. Distant. Steady.

Wind through gums. Light.

Tom's breathing from the chair in the next room. Even. Controlled.

Nothing else.

And yet.

She sat up slowly, feet finding the floor without sound. The kitchen was dark, lit only by moonlight filtering through the window. The plastic over the broken sitting room window lifted and fell with a soft, irregular tap.

Not wind.

Pressure.

Alice froze.

The tap came again. Slower this time. Testing.

She crossed to the bench and wrapped her fingers around the torch, not turning it on yet. The hallway stretched ahead of her - long, pale, the closed door at its end a darker rectangle in the dark.

Then she heard it.

The scrape of stone.

Not footsteps. Not wood.

Stone on stone, slow and deliberate, from the outside wall beneath the sitting room window.

Someone was there.

Her pulse slowed instead of racing, clarity sharpening her senses. She moved to the back door and eased it open just enough to slip onto the verandah. The night air was cool, heavy with the scent of wet earth.

The sound came again - closer now.

Alice lifted the torch and snapped it on.

The beam cut across the sitting room wall.

A man stood there with his back half-turned, hand braced against the stone, fingers white with pressure. He wasn't holding a weapon. He wasn't running.

He was prying.

"Stop," Alice said.

He startled, spinning toward the light. Younger than she'd expected. Early twenties, maybe. Sweat on his brow, fear in his eyes that hadn't learned how to be cruelty yet.

He bolted.

"Tom!" she shouted.

Footsteps pounded from inside the house as Tom burst onto the verandah. The young man ran for the trees, slipping once in the damp grass before disappearing into the scrub.

Tom swore softly and took two steps after him, then stopped.

"No," Alice said, breathless. "Let him go."

Tom turned, eyes sharp. "Alice—"

"He wanted something specific," she said. "And he didn't get it."

Tom's gaze flicked to the wall. To the stone beneath the sitting room window.

Something was different.

A faint line ran between two stones - not fresh paint, not damage - but a seam that had been worked, disturbed.

Tom stepped closer, running his fingers over it. "There's a cavity here."

Alice's stomach dropped.

"He wasn't trying to scare me," she said slowly. "He was trying to retrieve something."

They stared at the wall together, the implications settling heavy and undeniable.

"Whatever's hidden there," Tom said quietly, "he's been sent to get it before you find it."

Alice swallowed, the weight of choice pressing down on her.

"Then we don't wait for daylight," she said.

Tom looked at her - really looked - and nodded once. "All right."

They went back inside and gathered tools - nothing dramatic, just what the house offered. An old pry bar from the shed. A torch with fresh batteries. Gloves stiff with age.

Alice stood in front of the stone wall again, heart steady now, fear replaced by purpose.

"This is the trap," she said. "The thing he's been protecting."

Tom positioned the torch so the light fell cleanly across the seam. "Then let's see what the land's been holding."

Alice slid the pry bar into the narrow gap and leaned her weight into it.

Stone shifted.

Just a fraction.

Enough to change everything.

# CHAPTER TWENTY-THREE

The stone came free with a sound like a sigh.

Not dramatic. Not loud. Just the soft scrape of ancient mortar giving way after years of pressure. Alice steadied it as it shifted, easing it out and lowering it carefully to the floor. The cavity behind it yawned dark and narrow, no wider than her forearm.

Tom angled the torch inside.

Paper.

Not loose sheets - bundled. Wrapped in oilcloth gone stiff with age, edges darkened but intact. And beneath that, something heavier. Metal.

Alice's breath left her in a slow, careful exhale. "He knew."

Tom nodded. "Or his father did."

She reached in, fingers brushing the oilcloth. It was cold, gritty with stone dust. She drew it out slowly, as though speed might break the spell holding it together. The bundle landed on the table with a soft thud, followed by a smaller object wrapped separately.

Tom closed the stone cavity again - not sealing it, just hiding the absence for now - and turned back to her.

"Open it," he said.

Alice peeled the oilcloth back layer by layer. Inside were documents, thicker than the ones in the chest. Deeds. Signed affidavits. Survey sketches with official stamps pressed deep enough to leave scars in the paper.

Her hands trembled now. Not fear.

Recognition.

"This was never meant to disappear," she whispered. "It was meant to be hidden until someone needed it."

Tom picked up one of the documents and scanned it, his expression sharpening with every line. "This isn't just proof the fence was wrong. This shows intent. Coordination."

Alice lifted the smaller bundle and unwrapped it.

A key.

Old. Heavy. Numbered.

She stared at it. "A safe."

Tom's eyes flicked to her. "Where?"

She didn't answer immediately. She was already moving, crossing the hallway to the closed room, kneeling in front of the chest. She pushed it aside completely this time, running her hand along the back wall.

There.

A faint outline in the timber panelling. Not obvious unless you knew to look. She pressed the key into the lock and turned.

The panel opened.

Inside was a small wall safe, the metal dulled but solid. Alice hesitated only a second before opening it.

More papers.

And a notebook.

Handwritten. Her grandfather's hand - no mistaking it now. Pages filled with dates, names, observations. Who knew. Who looked away. Who threatened. Who stayed silent.

Alice sank back onto her heels, the weight of it hitting her all at once.

"He tried," she said, voice breaking despite herself. "He tried to do something with this."

Tom crouched beside her. "And now you can."

She flipped to the last page.

A single sentence, written more heavily than the rest.

*The land will tell the truth when the water rises.*

Alice closed her eyes.

Outside, the creek surged softly, still swollen, still honest.

She stood slowly, notebook clutched to her chest, and looked at Tom. "This ends it."

Tom nodded. "And it starts something else."

A sound echoed from outside then - not footsteps, not stone.

A car door.

Alice and Tom exchanged a look.

"This isn't him," Tom said quietly. "Too late. Too public."

They moved to the front window together.

A patrol car idled at the gate, headlights low. Helen Price stepped out, posture alert but not urgent.

Alice exhaled.

When Helen entered the house moments later, her gaze went straight to the table. To the documents. To the notebook in Alice's hands.

"You found it," she said.

Alice nodded. "Everything."

Helen took the notebook carefully, reading just enough to understand the shape of it. Her jaw tightened.

"This," she said quietly, "changes the entire story."

Alice met her eyes. "Then tell it properly."

Helen nodded once. "I will."

As Helen left with copies and photographs and promises that would now have to be kept, the house felt different again - lighter, as though something long wedged into its bones had finally been eased free.

Alice leaned against the kitchen bench, exhaustion crashing over her now that there was space for it.

Tom stepped close, resting his forehead briefly against hers - not a declaration, not a demand. Just connection.

"You were right," he said quietly. "The land was keeping it safe."

Alice closed her eyes. "Until someone was ready to listen."

Outside, dawn began to edge into the sky.

And with it came the truth - no longer buried, no longer silent, and no longer able to be controlled.

# CHAPTER TWENTY-FOUR

By the time the sun cleared the ridge, Taravale was already awake.

Not with noise - with movement. Utes on roads earlier than usual. Doors opening, then not quite closing again. People standing a little longer than necessary at gates and verandahs, watching the direction of the Gordon place as if the land itself might offer commentary.

Alice felt it in her bones as she stood at the kitchen window, notcbook now gone, papers copied and catalogued, the house strangely bare without the weight of its secrets pressing in from every wall.

"You all right?" Tom asked quietly.

She nodded. "I think so. Just... recalibrating."

A vehicle approached - slower than Gavin's had been, more deliberate. When it stopped at the gate, Alice recognised it instantly.

Senior Sergeant Mitchell. Not a Taravale local. Regional.

Helen stepped out behind him.

Alice's shoulders eased.

They came inside without ceremony. Mitchell took in the house with a practised eye - the patched window, the disturbed stonework, the papers spread neatly on the table.

"You did well to document," he said. Not praise. A statement of fact.

Alice met his gaze. "I just didn't want it twisted."

Mitchell nodded. "It won't be."

He turned to Tom. "You Callaghan?"

"Yes."

"Your name comes up in the notebook," Mitchell continued evenly. "Not as a participant."

Tom didn't flinch. "I figured."

"As a witness," Mitchell finished. "Repeatedly."

Tom exhaled once, slow and steady.

Mitchell opened his folder and slid out a map - newer, clean- lined, official. He laid it over the old one Alice had been studying for days. The creek lines matched.

"This," he said, tapping the page, "is what makes this criminal rather than civil. The intimidation. The deliberate concealment. The attempted retrieval last night."

Alice's jaw tightened. "Gavin didn't do that himself."

"No," Mitchell agreed. "But he directed it."

"And his father?" Alice asked.

Mitchell's expression shifted - something like regret, maybe. "Deceased. But not absolved."

Alice absorbed that in silence.

Helen spoke then, her voice quieter. "We'll be speaking to a few people today. Some of them won't enjoy it."

Tom's mouth twitched faintly. "Taravale doesn't enjoy daylight."

Mitchell closed the folder. "It's going to get loud for a while."

Alice nodded. "I can handle loud."

Mitchell studied her for a moment. "I believe you."

When they left, the house felt emptier - but not hollow. Purpose had replaced pressure.

By midday, the first call came.

A solicitor. City-based. Referred by Helen. Calm. Efficient. Very interested.

Then another.

Then Mara, pulling up in the van, expression fierce. "You've broken the internet," she announced, handing Alice a coffee. "Local Facebook group's in meltdown."

Alice laughed despite herself. "That didn't take long."

"No," Mara agreed. "Truth never does, once it's loose."

In the afternoon, Tom walked the boundary again - not to guard it, but to see it properly for the first time. Alice followed, boots sinking into drying mud, the land still reshaping itself underfoot.

"There," Tom said, stopping near the creek. "That bend."

Alice nodded. "That's where the line always was."

"And always will be."

They stood together, the water glinting in the sun, no fence to interrupt its logic.

Alice felt it then - not victory, not relief. Something quieter and deeper.

Completion.

"I didn't come back for this," she said softly.

Tom looked at her. "But you were the one who could finish it."

She turned toward the house - stone walls catching the light now, no longer half-hidden in shadow.

"Maybe," she said. "Or maybe the land just waited until someone stayed."

As the afternoon wore on, Taravale shifted around them - adjusting, resisting, reckoning.

And somewhere not far away, a man who had always believed himself untouchable was discovering what it felt like to have the ground give way beneath him.

The land had chosen.

And this time, it hadn't chosen him.

# CHAPTER TWENTY-FIVE

The arrest didn't happen with sirens.

It happened quietly, the way Taravale preferred things - contained, controlled, almost polite. Alice learned about it from Mara, who pulled up at the gate just before dusk, engine still running, eyes bright with a mix of relief and disbelief.

"They've taken him in," she said. "Gavin. Not overnight - questioning. Helen says it's only the beginning."

Alice closed her eyes briefly and let that settle. Not satisfaction. Not relief. Just the weight of inevitability finally finding its place.

Tom, standing beside her, nodded once. "That's how it starts."

Mara shifted, lowering her voice. "People are rattled. Some are angry. Some are pretending this has nothing to do with them."

Alice gave a small, tired smile.

After Mara left, the house felt unusually still.

Not tense. Not watchful.

Finished.

Alice walked through it slowly, room by room, noticing things she'd missed in the press of fear and purpose. The way light fell across the kitchen table in the late afternoon. The faint smell of smoke still clinging to the stone. The sitting room window patched but holding.

She stopped in the closed room last.

The chest sat open now, empty of secrets, its purpose fulfilled. The wall panel hung ajar, the safe bare. The room felt... ordinary. Just a room again.

That surprised her most.

Tom appeared in the doorway, leaning against the frame. "You okay?"

"Yes," she said, after a moment. "I think this is what it feels like when something stops chasing you."

He smiled faintly. "It takes some getting used to."

They ate dinner as the sun dropped behind the ridge - nothing special, just food and quiet conversation that didn't circle danger for once. Outside, the bush resumed its evening chorus, untroubled by human affairs.

Afterward, they sat on the verandah, the air cooling, the sky deepening into indigo. Fireflies flickered near the creek, brief sparks of life that didn't ask permission to exist.

Alice rested her elbows on the railing. "I was always going to leave again," she said quietly. "After the estate was settled."

Tom didn't answer right away.

She continued, voice steady. "I don't know if that's true anymore."

He turned toward her fully then. "You don't have to decide tonight."

"I know." She smiled softly. "But I like that I could."

They sat in companionable silence, the land stretching out before them - honest, reshaped, unconcerned with who claimed it now.

Later, when darkness fully claimed the valley, Alice locked the doors out of habit, then paused.

She unlocked the back one again.

Tom raised an eyebrow. "You sure?"

"Yes," she said. "For the first time, I am."

The house didn't object.

It settled around them easily, stone and timber holding without strain.

And somewhere deep beneath it all, the land released the last of what it had been keeping.

Not because it was forced to.

But because it was finally safe to let it go.

# CHAPTER TWENTY- SIX

The morning felt earned.

Sunlight spilled across the paddocks without hurry, warming the stone walls in a way that felt almost deliberate. Alice woke to the sound of birds arguing in the gums and the low murmur of Tom's voice somewhere near the shed. No alarms. No sirens. No tight coil of dread waiting behind her ribs.

Just morning.

She dressed and stepped onto the verandah, barefoot, the timber cool beneath her feet. The creek glinted between the trees, no longer swollen, its banks holding steady as if they'd always known how to do this.

Tom looked up from where he was stacking timber. "Sleep?"

"Yes," she said, surprised at how true it was. "Properly."

"Good."

They worked side by side for a while without speaking - the easy rhythm of shared space settling in naturally. Alice swept glass remnants from beneath the sitting room window. Tom checked hinges, tightened a latch that had always been loose but never urgent enough to fix.

Later, Helen called.

"Charges are being prepared," she said. "It'll take time. Statements. Depositions. But it's moving."

Alice leaned against the kitchen bench, sunlight warm on her back. "Thank you."

"You did the hard part," Helen replied. "You stayed."

When the call ended, Alice stood quietly for a moment, absorbing the word.

Stayed.

Tom watched her from the table. "Everything okay?"

"Yes," she said slowly. "I think... this is the part where the noise fades."

He smiled faintly. "And the consequences begin."

By mid-morning, the solicitor arrived - city accent, sharp suit, eyes already cataloguing the house and the land beyond it. They sat at the kitchen table with documents spread neatly between them, sunlight stripping them of their drama.

"This will be contested," the solicitor said calmly. "But the evidence is strong. Very strong."

Alice nodded. "I'm not in a hurry."

"That's good."

After the solicitor left, Alice walked the boundary alone.

She followed the creek line, boots sinking lightly into damp earth, hands brushing tall grass. The land felt different now - not altered so much as acknowledged. No fence interrupted its logic. No markers insisted on a version of truth that didn't fit.

She stopped where the creek bent sharply, water curling around stone and root.

Here.

She could feel it - the quiet certainty of place. Not ownership. Belonging.

Tom found her there an hour later. He didn't speak at first, just stood beside her, both of them facing the water.

"I used to think leaving was the bravest thing I ever did," Alice said finally. "Now I'm not so sure."

Tom glanced at her. "Maybe bravery changes shape."

She smiled at that.

They walked back toward the house together, the stone walls catching the afternoon light, the windows open, the doors unguarded.

That evening, Alice sat at the table and began writing.

Not affidavits. Not statements.

A letter.

Not to the town. Not to the Millsons.

To herself.

She wrote about leaving, and about returning. About silence mistaken for peace. About land that remembered even when people chose not to.

When she finished, she folded the page carefully and placed it in the now- empty chest.

Not as a secret.

As a marker.

Outside, the light softened into dusk, and Taravale settled into itself once more - changed, unsettled, but honest.

Alice stood in the doorway and watched the day end, feeling the unfamiliar, steady weight of something she hadn't expected to find here again.

Home.

# CHAPTER TWENTY-SEVEN

The town meeting filled the hall beyond capacity.

Alice stood near the back with Tom, the smell of dust and old timber thick in the air, the low murmur of voices pressing in from all sides. Folding chairs scraped across the floor as people shifted, settling into places that felt suddenly political. Familiar faces looked different here - less sure, less protected by routine.

Helen stood at the front beside Senior Sergeant Mitchell, papers clipped neatly to a board that looked too official for the room. The hum of conversation dipped as she raised her hand.

"This isn't a trial," Helen said evenly. "And it isn't a spectacle. It's information."

A ripple moved through the crowd.

Alice felt Tom's shoulder brush hers - steady, present.

Helen continued. "There's been a long-standing discrepancy between surveyed boundaries and natural boundaries along the creek. That discrepancy has now been formally documented."

Someone near the front shifted uncomfortably.

Mitchell spoke next, voice carrying easily. "There has also been evidence of intimidation, concealment of records, and attempted interference with an investigation. That matter is ongoing."

A murmur. Louder now.

A man stood. "Are you saying people here are criminals?"

Mitchell didn't hesitate. "I'm saying actions have consequences, regardless of how long they've been normalised."

Alice felt the weight of that sentence land.

Another voice cut in - sharp, defensive. "This town's always sorted its own problems."

Helen's gaze found the speaker. "That only works when the town is honest."

Silence followed.

Alice didn't intend to speak.

She hadn't come to make a statement or defend herself or ask for understanding. But when Helen's eyes found her - not inviting, just acknowledging - she realised staying quiet now would be its own kind of choice.

She stepped forward.

The room shifted.

"I didn't come back to accuse anyone," Alice said, voice carrying without effort. "I came back to settle an estate. What I found wasn't just paperwork - it was proof that silence had been mistaken for agreement."

A woman in the front row nodded slowly.

Alice went on. "The land didn't change. We did. And some of us benefited from pretending it hadn't."

A man stood abruptly, face flushed. "You think you're better than us because you left?"

Alice met his gaze calmly. "No. I think leaving saved me from learning how to look away."

The words landed harder than she expected.

She took a breath. "This isn't about punishment. It's about correction. About letting the truth sit where it belongs."

She stepped back then, heart steady, hands quiet at her sides.

The room didn't erupt.

It didn't applaud.

It absorbed.

People looked at each other differently now - not accusing, not united. Thinking.

Afterward, outside under the wide night sky, people lingered in small clusters. Some avoided her. Some nodded. A few stopped to speak - cautiously, sincerely.

Mara found her near the edge of the crowd. "You did good."

Alice smiled faintly. "I didn't plan to."

"Best kind," Mara replied.

Tom stood beside her as the hall lights dimmed behind them. "You didn't ask them to choose."

"No," Alice said. "I let them."

They walked back to the ute together, the road quiet, the gumtrees dark against the stars.

At the farmhouse later, Alice unlocked the door and paused.

"This doesn't feel temporary anymore," she said.

Tom looked at her, something warm and certain in his eyes. "No. It doesn't."

Inside, the house welcomed them without ceremony.

Stone. Timber. Light.

No secrets left to hold.

Only space for what came next.

# CHAPTER TWENTY-EIGHT

The paperwork took longer than anyone expected.

Not because it was complicated - the truth rarely was - but because it had been delayed for so long that it now had to pass through too many hands. Alice learned the rhythm of it quickly. Forms. Calls. Waiting. The strange fatigue that came from momentum slowed by process.

She didn't mind.

Taravale shifted around her in small, observable ways. The coffee van parked closer to the hall now, less tucked away. The pub conversations changed tone - quieter, more thoughtful. People stopped lowering their voices when she walked past. Some still avoided her, but avoidance had lost its edge. It felt less like judgement and more like adjustment.

The house settled too.

Tom replaced the sitting room window properly, timber and glass fitted clean and solid. The words that had once been painted on the stone were gone now. The wall bore no scar. Stone rarely did.

One afternoon, Alice found herself in the shed, sorting through old tools she didn't remember using but somehow knew where to place. She held a rusted fence staple in her palm, its curve familiar, its purpose finished.

"Throw it?" Tom asked from the doorway.

She considered it, then shook her head. "No. I'll keep it."

"For what?"

She smiled faintly. "Perspective."

They worked until the light shifted gold, then walked the boundary together - not checking, not guarding. Just walking.

At the creek bend, Alice stopped again.

"Surveyor confirmed it today," she said. "Officially."

Tom nodded. "It always was."

"Yes," she said. "But now it's recognised."

She crouched and pressed her hand to the damp earth, letting the coolness seep into her skin. It grounded her in a way nothing else had.

"You staying?" Tom asked quietly.

She looked up at him - really looked - the man who had known this land without trying to own it, who had stayed without needing to justify it.

"Yes," she said. "I think I am."

He didn't smile. He didn't celebrate.

He just nodded, like this was something he'd been ready to hear whenever she was ready to say it.

That night, Alice lay in bed listening to the house breathe - not holding its breath, not waiting. Simply existing. The creek murmured. The gums shifted. The world felt large and steady again.

For the first time since she'd returned, nothing felt unresolved.

And for the first time in a very long time, Alice let herself imagine a future that didn't require escape.

# EPILOGUE

The land looked different in winter.

Not softer - clearer.

Frost lay thin across the paddocks in the early mornings, silvering grass and fence posts that now followed the creek's honest line. The gumtrees shed bark in pale ribbons that curled at Alice's feet as she walked, the sound sharp and clean in the cold air.

The farmhouse held the season well.

Fireplaces were lit properly now, smoke rising straight and sure from the chimneys. The damp rooms stayed damp, the light rooms stayed bright. The house no longer felt like it was waiting to be understood. It simply existed - contradictions intact.

Alice learned its rhythms again, not as a child, not as a visitor, but as someone who stayed long enough for patterns to matter.

The case moved slowly, as cases did. Statements. Hearings. Settlements that made headlines without ever naming the quiet compromises beneath them. Gavin Millson's name appeared in print once, then less. His family's influence thinned, not dramatically - just enough.

Taravale adjusted.

It always had.

One afternoon, Alice stood at the creek bend with Tom, boots muddy, breath fogging in the air. The water ran steady, unbothered by paperwork or memory.

"I used to think the land needed protecting," she said.

Tom glanced at her. "From people?"

"From forgetting," she replied. "Turns out it was people who needed reminding."

He smiled faintly at that.

They walked back toward the house together, the stone walls catching the last of the sun. Light filled the kitchen. The hallway stretched, no longer ominous. The closed room remained open now -

just another part of the house, holding nothing it wasn't meant to.

That night, Alice locked the doors out of habit, then stopped herself.

She left one unlocked.

Not because she was reckless.

Because she understood the difference between fear and vigilance now.

Outside, the creek kept running.

The gumtrees stood, patient witnesses to everything that passed beneath them.

And inside the old stone house at Taravale, the land no longer kept its secrets.

It had given them back.

# AUTHOR'S NOTE

*What the Land Keeps* began as a story about inheritance.

Not money. Not property. But the things passed down quietly - silence, loyalty, fear, and the belief that keeping the peace is the same as doing the right thing.

Taravale is fictional, but its truths are not. Every small town has lines drawn long before we arrive, stories repeated until they feel inevitable, and moments when someone decides whether to stay quiet or speak.

This book is for the people who return. For the ones who stay. And for the land that remembers even when we try not to.

Thank you for walking Taravale with Alice and Tom. The story continues in **What The Land Leaves.**

# ABOUT THE AUTHOR

Emily Fraser writes rural romantic suspense set in Australia, where landscape, silence, and human connection shape the story as much as plot.

Her Taravale Series explores land, memory, and the quiet consequences of long-held secrets.

What the Land Keeps is her debut novel.